TEN SORRY TALES

MICK JACKSON

TEN SORRY TALES

illustrated by David Roberts

ff
faber and faber

First published in 2005
by Faber and Faber Limited
3 Queen Square London WC1N 3AU

Typeset by Faber and Faber Limited
Printed in England by Mackays of Chatham plc, Chatham, Kent

A CIP record for this book
is available from the British Library

ISBN 0–571–22548–9

2 4 6 8 10 9 7 5 3 1

Ten Sorry Tales

Contents

Contents

The Pearce sisters

Lol and Edna Pearce liked to keep their own company, which was just as well as their nearest neighbour lived nine miles away. Their tired old shack clung to the rocks right down by the shingle. Every room rattled with its own individual draughts and breezes and at high tide the waves came knocking at the door. But every now and again the sun cracked through the clouds, the rain abated and the wind would drop to a Force 5 or 6. Then the sisters would hike down the beach in search of driftwood and drag it back, to feed the stove and generally patch up their cabin where bits had fallen off.

They did their best to scrape a living from the sea's secret bounty. Six days a week they'd take their boat out and lift their nets to see what'd fetched up in them. Most of what they caught they ate; the rest they hung up in their smokehouse. After a few days in that black place, even the whitest flesh would turn an oily yellow and begin to take on the rich, sweet reek of tar. And once a fortnight the Pearce sisters would wrap their kippers and smoked mackerel and Finny haddock in old newspaper and head into town, to try and raise enough money to pay for one or two of life's little luxuries, such as bread or salt or tea.

One cold, wet Wednesday, Lol was up on the roof, nailing a scrap of wood over a hole where the rain had been making a nuisance and Edna was round the back, gutting and cleaning that morning's catch. Lol hammered the last nail into place, turned to make her way back to the ladder and happened to glance across the bay. It was a rare day when there was a single thing between the shore and the horizon but on that cold, wet Wednesday she thought she caught a glimpse of something out among the waves. She stopped and waited for the sea to flex its muscles. And after a while she saw for certain what she'd only glimpsed a moment before – a thirty-footer on its side, with some poor fellow clinging to it for all he was worth.

'Edna,' she called down to her sister, 'get the boat.'

Lol and Edna were tough old birds – used to lugging buckets and lobster pots up and down the place – and in a matter of minutes they had their boat down the beach and out on the water and their big, strong hands were hauling back the oars.

Lol kept an eye on the stricken boat over her shoulder as it swung in and out of view.

'You think he's drowned yet?' called out Edna.

'Not quite,' said Lol.

They cleared the top of that last wave just as the boat went under and began slowly rolling towards its watery grave. Its exhausted owner wasn't far behind. He'd gone down twice and was about to go down a third time – had

4

kicked and thrashed all the life right out of him. His eyes
rolled back in his head, his mouth fell open and with one
last kick and punch he sank beneath the waves.

The Pearces reached the spot where they'd last seen him
and Lol thrust her arm down into the sea and had a root
about. She shook her head at Edna and rolled her sleeve
right up to her shoulder. Then she delved back in, dug
down even deeper and when she finally sat back and pulled
her arm out of the water she had the half-drowned man by
the scruff of the neck.

They got him ashore, dropped him down on the pebbles
and started pumping. They must have pumped the best
part of a gallon of seawater out of him. Then Lol picked
him up, threw him over her shoulder and all three of them
went indoors.

On the whole, they thought him quite a reasonable-
looking fellow, with all his own teeth and a fine head of
dark-brown hair. In short, he was the kind of man the
Pearce sisters rarely got to see at such close quarters, so
they made the most of him being unconscious and had a
good strong look at him. They hung his sodden clothes by
the fire and rubbed him down with an old rag of a towel.
Then they wrapped him up in Edna's pink dressing gown
and pulled a pair of Lol's old socks on him to keep him
warm.

They mopped his brow as he lay stretched out on their
sofa. Combed his hair, just as if he was a doll. And they

were both still right up close and looking him over when he suddenly coughed and opened his eyes.

Now, there's no denying that Lol and Edna Pearce had passed their prime a few years earlier. The sisters had lived a long and arduous life. Their cheeks were blasted by the sea and wind, their hands were rough, their hair was matted. Their clothes were creased and greased from all the fish they'd rubbed up against. So when the half-drowned man opened his eyes it must have come as quite a shock to have both Pearces peering at him, when, to be fair, either one would have been more than enough.

'We had to pump you,' said Edna, and gave him a toothless smile.

The fellow's eyes darted to left and right. He was like a cornered animal – like a rabbit caught in a trap. He looked down and saw how he had been clad in Edna's old dressing gown. He looked back up at the sisters and let out a high-pitched scream.

In his defence, he was probably still a little disorientated – still had the odd pint of saltwater sloshing round his head. He leapt off the sofa, headed for the door and almost ripped it off its hinges. Then he was off – out on to the beach and weaving down the shingle, tripping and stumbling in his haste to get away.

The sisters stood and watched from their doorstep, quite bewildered. And that may well have been that, had the fellow not stopped at what he wrongly considered to be a safe distance and, still wearing Edna's dressing gown, raised an accusatory finger at the women who had just saved his life. A stream of insults came pouring out of him – a bilious rant, so crude and lewd that all the seagulls (not exactly known for their modesty) hung their heads in shame. Then the fellow turned and went back to stumbling down the beach.

Not surprisingly, Lol and Edna Pearce were a bit put out by the young man's behaviour, but Lol took extra umbrage as she'd been the one to spot him and the one to pull him out. She felt her chest fill up with righteous indignation. She adjusted her cardigan and set off after him.

He must have heard her footsteps in the shingle. Must have heard her closing in on him. He may even have had time to regret his little outburst. Certainly, old Lol Pearce was better at making her way across the pebbles and in a matter of minutes she was on him. She grabbed his shoulder, spun him round and lamped him. He went down and showed no immediate signs of getting up again.

Lol stood over him like a champion boxer and called out to her sister.

'Get the boat,' she said.

They threw him back almost exactly where they found him. Then rowed the quarter mile or so back to the shore. And, in truth, they thought no more about it, until a day or two later, when they were combing the beach for

7

driftwood and found him lying in the wash, with Edna's old dressing gown spread all about him and still buttoned under his chin. They stopped and looked at him for a minute. He seemed quite peaceful. There was never any debate as to what to do with him. They simply dropped their driftwood, picked him up by his arms and ankles and carefully carried him back to their shack.

For a couple of hours he sat in one of the chairs out on the verandah, as if he'd just nodded off after a heavy lunch. Then Lol suggested they bring him inside, in case somebody happened to see him. And from that point on he became a permanent fixture. Something they wouldn't have swapped for all the tea in China or all the fish in the sea.

They found the clothes he'd left behind on his previous visit and dressed him up in them. Then they sat him in an easy chair. He looked perfectly happy gazing into the fire, and Lol and Edna agreed that when he wasn't running up and down and generally causing a commotion he was the very model of good company.

A day or two passed. The sisters went about their business. And in the evenings all three of them sat before the fire. Edna said how nice it was to have a man around the house. Lol agreed, but said that if they hoped to keep him they'd better consider how to stop him going off.

They removed his clothes again, carried him round the back and laid him out on the same stone slab on which they prepared their haddock and mackerel. Edna sharpened her knife, cut him up the middle and Lol helped to take his insides out. They took the twine they used to mend their nets and sewed him back together. Then they hung him in the smokehouse for a week or so, looking in on him now and again, to see how he was doing, until they were certain he was done all the way through.

For the first couple of weeks they sat him in the armchair. Then they perched him on a stool, with his hands on the keys of the old upright piano their mother used to play when she was still alive. It had long since seized up from all the salty air but they were both very fond of it and liked it even more with him sitting at it, as if he was about to launch into some old song from the music hall.

The first fellow to join him was some chap from the local council who came knocking on the door to ask if they had the proper planning permission for all the sheds and home-made extensions they'd added to their house. Lol and Edna took the fellow out in their boat to show him how things looked from a distance and with one little push he was over the side. Sure enough, a day or so later, they found him washed up, not a hundred yards from where the first one came in. His spectacles were missing but his suit was more or less intact.

Their third guest was a plain old nosey parker who just happened to come across their cottage and strode down the path to have a snoop about. He didn't even get to have the trip out into the bay before visiting the smokehouse. He'd crept up to the shack and had his nose pressed up against the kitchen window when it suddenly flew open. Lol grabbed him by the lapels of his jacket, dragged him in and dunked him in the washing-up. For a man who'd held such sway in his own household it was a most undignified way to go.

The fourth victim was a blameless rambler who made the fatal error of knocking on the Pearces' door to ask for directions. He had a little beard, which the sisters were not particularly keen on, but they were desperate to find one more man, to complete the set. They led him down to the sea to point out the path that he was after, and as the two of them stood up to their thighs in water and held him under, they watched his Ordnance Survey map slowly flap and tumble down the beach.

They gave him a shave before they smoked him. Now he sits in the Pearces' parlour, with the other three. They read their books, play cards and sit at the piano, like exhibits in a strange museum. Four drowned men, all nice and quiet, biding their time with Lol and Edna Pearce.

The boy who fell asleep

He'd always been known as a bit of a sleepy-head, which is the kind of reputation that can follow a boy around. It would take him an age to wake up in the morning and he was forever nodding off in the afternoon. He would just be staring out of the classroom window and feel his eyes getting heavy and the next thing he'd be conked-out, with his head on his desk, which didn't go down at all well with his teacher – a bald, old coot called Mister Winter, who took great pleasure in throwing chalk at any child not paying proper attention to what he had to say.

It wasn't as if he was especially fond of sleeping. Nodding off, in his experience, could be a most uncomfortable business, like a tug-of-war between staying awake and falling asleep. He just had the sort of mind that liked to wander and, once it got wandering, always seemed to lead him into unconsciousness.

He was lucky enough not to have any brothers or sisters, which meant there was no one constantly bossing him about the place or getting under his feet. There was just his father, who was either out at work or slumped in an armchair reading his newspaper and his mother, who never seemed to sit still for two minutes at a time.

The first real sign that there was anything the matter was when he went to bed at eight o'clock one Friday evening and was still fast asleep at half-past ten the following day. His mother had to sit him up and splash his face with cold water before getting any sense out of him. When he eventually came around he muttered something about being on a boat on a winding river. An oarless boat that had just been drifting, drifting all night long.

The following week he fell asleep in mid-geography. Mister Winter was pointing at a map of the world and talking about far-away places – the sort of talk which can easily exhaust a boy – when he felt his mind begin to wander and sleep to work its charms on him. By the time old man Winter noticed he was asleep there was no retrieving him. The chalk just bounced right off his head. And in the end, four classmates had to carry him home on a blackboard, like some casualty from sleep's battlefront.

His parents put him to bed and watched anxiously over him. Two full days went by before he finally surfaced – a bit groggy, but otherwise right as rain. He had a bath and a large fried breakfast and on the Monday morning was back at school, with a note from his mother apologizing for his behaviour and saying how he'd been a bit under the weather but was now most definitely on the mend.

His father went back to reading his paper. His mother returned to her chores. But their son's new habit of slipping into unwakeable sleep so worried his parents they became reluctant to get him to close his eyes at bedtime, when they had no way of knowing when he was going to open them up again.

One Thursday evening a couple of weeks later he sat and yawned by the fire for half an hour, before finally getting to his feet and shuffling off up the stairs. As soon as his head hit the pillow he knew that the most potent sort of sleep was moving in on him. He could feel its heavy tide tug at his very bones. He had no choice but to surrender to it. His body seemed to sink just like a stone. And as he went under he briefly wondered how long he'd be gone this time.

The moment his mother woke the following morning she knew something was wrong and that her son had slipped from her grasp. She rushed into his room and found him lying with the sheets all neat and flat around him, just the same as when she'd tucked him in the night before. She put her palm against his forehead – sleepy-warm. His breath was sleepy-sweet. She turned and called out to her husband.

'*John,*' she cried, '*he's gone again.*'

Lunchtime came and went with not the slightest prospect of him stirring. In the afternoon they called the doctor out. He checked the boy's pulse and opened up both eyelids, but found no sign of life in either one. In the doctor's opinion there were only two possible explanations. Either the boy had caught sleeping sickness (which was not very likely, as it is a Tropical Disease normally spread by the dreaded *tsetse fly*, which lives in the sort of far-away places Mister Winter had been pointing out on his map a few weeks before) or the boy was simply sound asleep, in which case the doctor thought it best just to keep an eye on him and let the sleep run its natural course.

For the first couple of weeks there was a steady stream of visitors. Aunts and uncles came by to have a look and to comfort his mother. Neighbours knocked on the door to see if there was any news. And one Monday, a school inspector paid a visit to make sure his missing pupil wasn't lounging around and generally enjoying himself when he could be stuck at school, staring out of the window and having Mister Winter throw chalk at him.

After a month his parents had to accept that this was not just some passing fancy and began to develop a little routine for their sleeping child. In the morning they rolled him on to his left side and in the afternoon they rolled him on to his right. Twice a week they changed his sheets and washed his pyjamas and every evening opened up the window to let some fresh air in. They sat him up, to wash his lifeless body and to spoon some soup into him. And, one way or another, they took care of all his other bodily functions which, for the sake of decency, we shall not go into here.

His mother and father made sure that either one of them was always within earshot, in case he suddenly woke

up and called out to them. And at the end of each day they
sat by his bed and talked, just like any normal family, as if
he might open his eyes and join in at any time.

As the years crept by the legend of the sleeping boy
spread right across the country and two or three times a
week some stranger would turn up on the doorstep asking
to have a peek at him or present some home-made remedy
which, they assured his parents, would have him back on
his feet in no time at all.

But only two people ever found their way into the boy's
company without being invited. One Sunday evening the
young twins from down the road managed to shimmy up
the drainpipe and slip into his bedroom when his mother
was busy downstairs. The twins were quite convinced that
he wasn't really sleeping and both had brought a pin to
prove their point. They stood at the foot of the bed and
watched his chest slowly rising and falling. They pulled
the bedclothes back and gazed at his two pale feet. They
nodded to one another. Then they pushed their pins into
him.

They expected him to leap up, with his eyes wide open,
but the sleeping boy didn't even flinch. When they removed
their pins, two beads of blood crept out and trickled down
his footsoles. Then the twins were suddenly horrified at
what they'd done and how deeply the boy was sleeping
and they both went charging down the stairs and out into
the street.

For ten long years the sleeping boy never left his bedroom. Every morning his parents rolled him on to his left side and every afternoon they rolled him on to his right. They fed and bathed him, trimmed his hair and did their best to draw him into conversation. Christmas Days and birthdays crept quietly by. And in all that time the only thing that ever found its way through to him was his mother's voice – just a few words now and again, which sounded muffled and dreadfully distant, as if he was deep inside a whale.

The rest of the time he was blissfully ignorant. He was locked away deep within himself. All except for one solitary occasion when he briefly grasped that he'd somehow muddled up being asleep with being awake. For one awful moment he understood that he was sleeping, without having the first idea how to bring himself around. He wanted to call out – to break the spell – but his cry for help was stuck deep in his sleeping body. Then another dream swept in, embraced him and drew him back into the deeper reaches of unconsciousness.

It was a long, slow hibernation, and it took its toll on the boy's poor mum and dad, who themselves began to drift around the place in their own half-waking state. Their hair turned grey from all the worry. Their dreams were full of pain and fear. But on one otherwise ordinary Sunday morning their suffering finally came to an end.

The boy's mother was quietly tidying his room around

him and sat on the bed for a moment, to catch her breath. She talked to her son, as she'd done a thousand times before, about whatever happened to be on her mind – all the little jobs that needed doing and how the summer was slowly coming around. She brushed his hair to one side with her fingers, kissed him on his forehead and rested her cheek against his sleeping face. She closed her eyes and whispered a few kind words to him, and was breathing in the smell of his hair when she thought she felt the flicker of an eyelash against her cheek. And when she sat back there was her son, with his eyes wide open, looking up at her.

She called out to the boy's father, who came running up the stairs even quicker than the neighbours' twins had once run down them. And he and his wife sat and stared at their son, who lay there, blinking and looking all around him, as if he had been washed up on some forgotten shore.

It took him a while to gather his senses and a good while longer to cobble together his first words. He opened his mouth, but his throat was as dry as bracken.

'I've been asleep,' he croaked.

He desperately wanted to get up but all his muscles had grown weak and withered. So his father took one arm around his shoulder, his mother took the other and between them they managed to get him to his feet. As he limped along he had the most peculiar feeling: either his parents had been busy shrinking or he'd been busy growing up.

In fact, he'd grown no more than most boys do between the ages of ten and twenty. When he fell asleep he was four foot six. When he awoke he was six foot two. He leant against the window ledge and looked out at the world he'd last seen ten years earlier. The birds were singing. The clouds slowly rolled across the sky. Then he turned and headed back towards his bed. On his way he passed a mirror and caught sight of some young man resting on the shoulders of his own mother and father. He stood – quite stunned – and stared at the young man, who stood and stared right back at him.

When word got out that he'd woken up the queue of well-wishers stretched right down the street. And when he was finally strong enough to go out on his own, people would run up to him and shake his hand and tell him how they never doubted that he'd eventually wake up again.

Once he'd fully recovered he decided to go back to school, to complete his education. The other children found it hugely entertaining to have a tall young man sitting among them, and for the first few days they kept looking over at him, to see if he'd nodded off again. But after a while they grew accustomed to his presence and treated him much like any other child.

Mister Winter had retired a couple of years earlier, when he'd grown too old to throw his chalk with any accuracy, and a young woman called Miss Hayes had taken his place.

Miss Hayes was roughly the same age as her new pupil. The boy's parents suggested he ask her out, but it didn't seem quite right somehow to be asking out one's teacher, and he never got around to it.

After a couple of terms he gave up on the whole idea of schooling and got a job on a nearby farm. He worked there most of his life and lived to a grand old age, but it wouldn't be true to say that he was happy. There were too many days when he felt profoundly out of sorts. He didn't like being in rooms when the doors were closed. He was afraid of the dark and in the summer he slept out in the garden, where he could look up and see the stars.

All too often he felt like a boy trapped inside a man's body. He could be dreadfully shy and sometimes had terrible trouble finding the right words for what he had to say. And when he closed his eyes at night he would sometimes wonder if that strange, fathomless sleep was waiting for him and whether he would ever again have to endure that awful feeling of being deep inside a whale.

A row-boat in the cellar

The most unusual thing about Mister Morris was the fact that he was missing a leg. It got blown off when he was a soldier a long, long time ago. He'd been sitting in a trench in the middle of nowhere when a shell came screaming out of a clear blue sky. The same terrible shell that blew Mister Morris's left leg off also killed his best friend Frank. One minute they were crouching in their trench, talking about cricket, the next minute young Frank was dead.

After the war, Mister Morris got a job in a hardware shop, selling screws and glues and nuts and bolts. If someone was hanging a door, he'd tell them what sort of hinge they needed. If they were putting up a shelf he'd tell them which brackets to buy. Whenever a customer bought a light bulb Mister Morris would insist on checking it. He'd slip the bulb out of its cardboard sleeve and twist it into a socket behind the counter. If it lit up he'd say, 'That's a good 'un.' If it didn't (which wasn't very often) he'd say, 'That's a bad 'un,' and throw it in the bin.

For forty-two years Mister Morris sold bottles of turps and methylated spirits and gave his customers advice on brushes and bradawls and brooms. He spent all day hobbling about the shop on his wooden leg (which had a shoe neatly fastened to the end of it), without uttering a single word of disgruntlement. He was a popular man – a mine of useful information. And when he finally retired the other members of staff took him out to dinner and gave him a watch for his waistcoat pocket, with an inscription which read, 'Time to put your foot up, old son.' At the end of the night Mister Morris shook hands with his old colleagues and hobbled off down the street. But when he woke on the Monday morning he decided that he was going to need a project to keep him occupied.

For some people, retirement can be a bit of a shock to the system. They suddenly find they have far too much time on their hands. Some stay in bed, trying to catch up on all the sleep they think they've missed out on. Some study. Some watch daytime TV. But it can be hard changing the habits of a lifetime. They wake up early, even though they didn't set the alarm. They miss the old routine. And the days can sometimes seem to stretch out before them like an empty, friendless place.

Some people miss the company of their old work-mates and begin to wish they'd never left their job. Mister Morris felt no such thing. But he knew he needed something to keep him busy, and began to wonder what sort of project he should set himself.

Every morning of his first week of retirement he made a pot of tea, boiled himself an egg, then walked along the

In the weeks that followed, Mister Morris did his best not to think about it, whilst actually thinking about it a great deal of the time. He went to the shops, cooked his dinner and listened to the radio but kept finding himself down in the cellar, staring at his stranded rowing boat.

One Wednesday evening he was walking by the river when he noticed how high the water was getting. There had been a lot of rain lately (which was not that unusual) and he thought no more about it until he was woken in the middle of the night by the sound of people shouting in the street. He stuck his head out of the window. All his neighbours were standing around in their pyjamas and wellingtons.

'It's the river, Mister Morris,' one of them called up to him. 'It's burst its banks.'

Mister Morris closed the window and hopped back into bed. He sat there for a couple of minutes, thinking. Then he strapped his wooden leg on, found his dressing gown and went down the stairs.

When he opened the door to his cellar he was confronted by a scene that both horrified and delighted him. Cardboard boxes and tins of varnish were floating in three feet of water. Jars of screws and bottles of beer were bobbing about the place. And in their midst, looking serene and stately, drifted Mister Morris's rowing boat.

He made a lasso out of a bit of old washing line, twirled it above his head once or twice and threw it in the

In the weeks that followed, Mister Morris did his best not to think about it, whilst actually thinking about it a great deal of the time. He went to the shops, cooked his dinner and listened to the radio but kept finding himself down in the cellar, staring at his stranded rowing boat.

One Wednesday evening he was walking by the river when he noticed how high the water was getting. There had been a lot of rain lately (which was not that unusual) and he thought no more about it until he was woken in the middle of the night by the sound of people shouting in the street. He stuck his head out of the window. All his neighbours were standing around in their pyjamas and wellingtons.

'It's the river, Mister Morris,' one of them called up to him. 'It's burst its banks.'

Mister Morris closed the window and hopped back into bed. He sat there for a couple of minutes, thinking. Then he strapped his wooden leg on, found his dressing gown and went down the stairs.

When he opened the door to his cellar he was confronted by a scene that both horrified and delighted him. Cardboard boxes and tins of varnish were floating in three feet of water. Jars of screws and bottles of beer were bobbing about the place. And in their midst, looking serene and stately, drifted Mister Morris's rowing boat.

He made a lasso out of a bit of old washing line, twirled it above his head once or twice and threw it in the

direction of the boat. Then Mister Morris slowly drew
his row-boat towards him, like a rancher drawing in some
wild-eyed horse. He gently eased himself off the stairs on
to the boat's broad cross-bench and, once he was settled,
carefully pushed himself away from the stairs. And for the
rest of the night Mister Morris rowed blissfully back and
forth between the walls of his flooded cellar, through all
the flotsam and jetsam of his life.

It wasn't much, but it was better than nothing. At least
he got to practice how to do his turns. Most of his
neighbours spent the next few days standing around
complaining and saying how they'd never get over it.
Meanwhile, Mister Morris was down in his cellar, finding
his sea legs, and might well have slept in his precious boat
if he hadn't thought it would be a bit uncomfortable.

By the Thursday afternoon it had more or less stopped
raining and, not long after, the water level began to fall.
Mister Morris rose early on the Saturday morning, hoping
to squeeze in another couple of hours' rowing, but opened
the cellar door to find the boat (and all his bits and pieces)
beached in several inches of mud.

It was a horrible mess, but Mister Morris rose to the
challenge, and as he scooped up the mud and wiped down
the walls he was already looking forward to the possibility
of other, even more disastrous floods. From that day
forward every drop of rain would lift his spirits. Every
black cloud would give him hope. He kept a close eye on

the river but it never really looked in any serious danger of coming over the top.

He decided to think ahead. It seemed highly likely that the river would flood around the same time the following year. If he could create a little more space in his cellar he would have more room to row about. So he embarked on a year-long programme of earth removal. He bought a pick and a brand-new barrow and started hacking away at the cellar wall. His first tunnel was five foot high and six foot wide and headed out under the street, where it soon came up against all sorts of drains and pipes and other obstacles. So Mister Morris started a second tunnel, which headed under his back garden, and on this his progress was both swift and sure.

He supported the tunnel roof with odd bits of timber he'd picked out of skips. On a typical day he might spend four or five hours tunnelling, then sleep for an hour or two. He would cook himself some dinner, then wait until nightfall. And in the early hours of the morning he would carry the buckets of earth up the stairs to his waiting barrow and wheel it off down the moonlit streets.

On the first few nights he dumped the earth in his neighbours' gardens but it was clear that there was a limit to how long he could get away with that. So he wheeled his barrow down to the river and tipped the soil into the water, where it sank without a trace. This was a much more practical way of going about things. Mister Morris thought that in time it might even help to raise the water level by an inch or two. Nobody seemed to mind an old man wandering around the place with a wheelbarrow after bedtime. A town's streets are surprisingly quiet between the hours of three and four a.m. Only once did Mister Morris have any trouble, when a police car pulled up alongside him as he emptied another barrow-load of earth into the river.

The policeman wound down his window and shone a torch into Mister Morris's face. He asked Mister Morris if he'd mind explaining what he was up to.

Mister Morris looked down into his empty barrow then back up at the policeman. 'I'm retired,' he said.

The policeman took a moment to chew this over. His own father had retired a couple of years earlier and was for ever getting up at half past five to do the hoovering. The policeman told Mister Morris to make sure he didn't wake anybody up whilst he was about his business. Then he wound his window back up and drove off into the night.

Progress continued at a steady rate. Five months after he first started Mister Morris estimated that the tunnel was approximately a quarter of a mile in length. If he could keep on at the same sort of pace he reckoned he'd be out of town and under Birch Hill by the time the rain came round again.

About a month before the floods were expected Mister

Morris tied his boat to the bottom banister to stop it being swept away. He grew more and more excited but one Tuesday night, after a hard day's digging, he was walking alongside the river when he noticed some activity up ahead. He got a bit closer and saw a dozen soldiers standing in a line between a lorry and the river, passing sandbags from man to man.

Mister Morris suddenly felt quite sick. He approached one of the soldiers on the riverbank and asked what they were doing.

'Don't you worry, sir,' the soldier told him. 'That river'll not be breaking its banks this year.'

The soldier took a bag of sand from his mate, dropped it on top of all the others and stamped it into place with his boot. Mister Morris looked at all the sandbags piled up along the edge of the river and the lorry-load of sandbags waiting to be piled on top of them and felt that chilly feeling sweep over his shoulders again.

He'd spent the best part of a year working on this project. Every day straight after breakfast he'd sat in his boat, imagining paddling down his own home-made tunnel. He'd even bought some greaseproof paper to wrap around his sandwiches and a flask for his tea. But now all the life seemed to suddenly drain right out of him. And all the effort he'd put into the tunnel seemed to catch him up. For the first time in his life he felt like an old man. A useless, worn-out piece of work.

Mister Morris stopped his digging. He took to his bed and listened to his radio. And all the time his mind was piled high with those blasted sandbags which were keeping the river at bay.

The following week the rain came, just as Mister Morris predicted. It lashed the windows and drummed on the roof of his unhappy house. He put on a raincoat and found his umbrella and went down to the river to see how high it was getting. The water swept by at quite a lick and came right up to the sandbags. If those soldiers hadn't put them there, Mister Morris thought, he'd be in his boat, paddling up and down that tunnel he'd spent all year hacking out of the ground.

It was starting to get dark. He looked at the sodden sandbags by his feet. Here and there the odd trickle of water seeped between them. Now, if only one or two sandbags happened to get knocked out of the way, Mister Morris thought to himself.

He gave one of them a little kick with his wooden leg, but couldn't get enough power behind it. He took his umbrella down and tried prodding at the sandbag with that instead. In truth, he wasn't making much of an impression when he had a funny feeling that he was being watched. He turned and found a man standing not far away, wrapped up in a raincoat. After a couple of moments the man took a step towards Mister Morris.

'Do you need a hand?' he said.

As he came a little closer, Mister Morris could see that the man was about the same age as himself, if not a little older. The fellow bent down, picked up one of the sandbags and handed it back to Mister Morris. Mister Morris took it and turned to throw it over his shoulder when another man, of similar vintage, suddenly appeared.

'I'll take that,' he said.

Within a minute there were a dozen of them, all working together. Twelve old men handing the sandbags down a chain, just like the soldiers who'd brought them in a few weeks before.

The first sign that their endeavours had been successful was when the man next to Mister Morris called out, 'That should do it,' and waved for everyone to get out of the way. A couple of sandbags slowly rolled aside under the weight of the water. Then the river seemed to suddenly sense a new course for itself, punched a hole right through the bank of sandbags and sent them tumbling all over the place.

Mister Morris hurried home just as fast as his leg would carry him. By the time he opened his cellar door there was at least two feet of water flushing straight down his tunnel and his boat was tugging at its leash.

He grabbed his torch and climbed into his row-boat, which was so eager to be on its way that Mister Morris found it impossible to untie the rope and had to cut it with a knife. Then he was off, racing down the rapids, down his dark, dark tunnel, with hardly time to catch his breath.

Mister Morris didn't get the chance to do much rowing. He was too busy trying to keep his boat from being smashed to smithereens. The walls flew by and when he wasn't guiding the boat between them he was shining his torch over his shoulder, to see how far he had to go.

It was quite a ride and one that Mister Morris wouldn't have missed for the world. It was the sort of exhilaration he rarely experienced behind the counter at the hardware shop. But just when he'd begun to thoroughly enjoy himself and to whoop and hear his own whoops echoing back at him, the boat began to slow and he found himself at the end of the tunnel where the water was boiling and raging from all the other water backed-up behind.

Mister Morris got hold of his oars and started rowing back towards his cellar. He rowed like mad but wasn't going anywhere. He was held in the grip of the floodwater, as it thrashed and buffeted his boat up against the tunnel wall.

Then he noticed that the water was still rising. For some reason he'd imagined that it would climb to a depth of a couple of feet, then simply stop. But the boat was being steadily lifted on the water, with Mister Morris inside, furiously rowing, until at last he found himself being pressed right up against the tunnel roof.

The water kept on coming and began to creep over the side of the boat. The torch went out, the water roared and churned around him and in that terrible watery darkness Mister Morris finally surrendered to his fate.

'It's not such a bad way to go,' he thought to himself. 'Drowning in my own tunnel, in my own home-made rowing boat.'

The water completely engulfed him. Mister Morris slumped forward.

'This is it,' he said out loud.

But at that last moment, when his whole life seemed to swim about him, the stubborn wall gave way and Mister Morris, his boat and the millions of gallons of water behind them were launched into what felt like the very heart of the earth.

When things eventually settled down and Mister Morris dared to sit up straight he found himself in unfamiliar surroundings. His boat was gently drifting in the middle of a vast underground lagoon. Vast stalagmites and stalactites reached up and down around the water's edges. And all the walls and the cavernous ceiling had a smooth and eerie sheen to them.

Mister Morris noticed several other boats drifting here and there in the distance. Each had a hurricane lamp hanging from a pole. One of the boats was slowly being paddled over towards him. When it finally came alongside, Mister Morris recognized the owner. It was the old fellow from the riverbank.

'Glad you could join us,' he told Mister Morris.

Mister Morris did his best to regain a little composure. 'That's very kind of you,' he said at last.

'You'll be needing a lantern,' the other fellow told him. 'To see where you're going.'

Mister Morris nodded. 'I know a shop where I can pick one up,' he said.

The other fellow smiled and started to turn his boat around.

'We tend to leave each other alone,' he said. 'But if you want a bit of company, just give me a wave.'

Mister Morris thanked him, then watched as the old fellow rowed off into a quiet stretch of that vast, milky lake.

'I should've brought some sandwiches,' Mister Morris thought to himself.

For the rest of his days, Mister Morris rowed on the lake on a regular basis. It gave him the chance for a little reflection. He also liked to think that the rowing kept him fit. And as he rowed he remembered his mother and father and the day they rowed on Lake Windermere. And, from time to time, he thought about his old friend Frank, who died in the war all those years ago.

The lepidoctor

A *coincidence* **is sometimes** just the world's way of getting your attention – a way of getting you to sit up and take notice once in a while. Some coincidences are so slight as to barely merit a raised eyebrow. Others carry such weight that, when acted upon accordingly, they have the power to change the course of your life.

The coincidence at the heart of this particular story is of quite considerable magnitude, not least for the boy and the butterflies involved. It has its origins one Saturday morning when Baxter Campbell paid a visit to the Houghton Museum – a place packed full of stuffed bears and birds and Paraguayan nose-flutes and various bits of bone and stone which had, at one time or another, been brought back from every corner of the world.

Baxter was himself an unusually cultured young fellow. In his bedroom he kept an old harmonium on which he would compose his own maudlin lullabies. On his bedside table sat a leather-bound collection of the poetry of Alfred Lord Tennyson. On his walls were pinned the paintings of Pieter Breughel and Hieronymus Bosch. All of the above he'd picked up for next to nothing in jumble sales and junk shops. Like his dad, Baxter found anything old or

43

second-hand peculiarly alluring. Old stuff had *history* to it. Old stuff had *character*.

When Baxter was still a baby he accompanied his father to every second-hand shop, street market and auction on his busy itinerary. So, long before he could walk or talk, Baxter was already familiar with the smell of mould and mothballs and the sight of grown men haggling over the sort of old books and clocks and china most people would just throw away.

These days, Baxter was old enough to go on his own to the same second-hand shops and flea markets his dad had introduced him to. And on Friday nights he and his dad liked nothing better than to sit by the fire and trawl through the small ads in the back of the local paper, circling any item they liked the sound of, such as 'Cast iron bedstead. A bit bent. Very heavy' or 'Large box of chemistry equipment – eg test tubes, pipettes, etc. Offers please.'

If there'd been a *Mrs* Campbell she might have had something to say about the cardboard boxes which lined the hallway and the stacks of books which clogged the stairs. But Baxter's mother had departed this world the same hour Baxter had entered it. Baxter's father had raised him on his own and early on the two of them had come to an agreement whereby Baxter's dad would store all his stopped clocks, Second World War memorabilia and railway paraphernalia in the basement and Baxter would have the use of the attic for his old adding machines and broken wirelesses.

On Saturday mornings Baxter liked to visit one of the local museums and have a look at some ancient pair of Roman underpants or the shin bone of some Neolithic Man. He liked to eat his lunch at the Turkish café and, in the afternoons, to call in at all the jumble sales he'd picked out of the paper the night before. On this particular Saturday Baxter stood in the Houghton Museum before a glass cabinet containing an old pair of handcuffs. They came from Bristol, apparently, and looked as if they weighed a ton. Baxter wondered what sort of crime you had to commit to find yourself wearing them and whether the same poor sod who'd been shackled by them had been whipped within an inch of his life by the cat-o'-nine-tails from the neighbouring cabinet.

Baxter walked on, past the polar bear, baring its teeth and raised up on its hind legs, past the row of Balinese slippers and the display of Moroccan board games and only paused when he came face to face with a poster which announced 'BUTTERFLY: a new exhibit by Milton Spufford' with a big black arrow pointing into the next room. As we have already established, Baxter Campbell was a cultivated boy and not the least bit intimidated by either Art or Culture. And as he still had plenty of time before his next appointment (a jumble sale up at the Methodist Church at one o'clock) he decided to follow the signs, passed through an archway and came out into a large white room.

What struck him first were the incredible colours – the colours and the actual size of the thing. Vivid blues, emerald greens and luminous turquoises all shimmered together in the two huge wings of a single vast butterfly which was so big it practically filled the whole of one wall.

Baxter was impressed, there was no denying it. The creature somehow managed to be both beautiful and monstrous at the same time. It was only as he walked towards it that he saw how that massive butterfly was actually made up of several hundred *real* butterflies which had been carefully arranged into something like a huge mosaic.

'Oi!' someone said.

Baxter jumped. Without realizing it, he'd walked right up to the butterfly and raised his index finger. An overweight security guard, standing about ten feet away, seemed quite prepared to bundle Baxter to the ground if necessary.

'No touching,' he said.

Baxter brought his hand down and went back to studying the individual butterflies. He could see the fine fur which covered their tiny bodies – the faint veins which wired their wings. One butterfly's wings were all chalky blues and whites, as dusty as powder paint. Another's were so black and glistened so wetly they looked as if they had just been dipped in ink.

Each was so pristine that Baxter was having trouble believing they weren't still living – as if they might have been specially trained to hang in formation all day long. It was a nice idea but one which promptly vanished when Baxter noticed the head of a pin in the middle of the butterfly right in front of him, then of every other butterfly, which held them to the wall.

Baxter was beginning to feel quite ill. He decided to leave the museum. On his way he passed a large photograph of Milton Spufford, the man who'd put together this weird work of art. He was standing on a hillside in baggy shorts, with a butterfly net in one hand and a large glass jar in the other. Underneath the photograph it said: 'Once caught, the butterfly is dropped into the "killing jar" where the smell of crushed laurel leaves soon lulls the creature into a permanent sleep.'

Baxter was completely bamboozled. He'd come across plenty of dead animals in his time – tatty fruit bats . . . over-stuffed walruses . . . rhinos with paper-thin skin – but they'd all been caught and stuffed at least a hundred years earlier. The idea of someone catching and killing butterflies these days just seemed plain stupid. You'd have thought there were few enough butterflies to begin with, without going round sticking pins in them.

He left the museum and did his best to forget about those beautiful dead butterflies, but wasn't particularly successful. And for the rest of the afternoon as he rummaged at his various jumble sales that monstrous butterfly kept looming up in his imagination and threatened to overshadow the whole weekend.

A couple of weeks later Baxter paid his monthly visit to Monty Eldridge's Second-Hand Emporium. Monty liked to think of his establishment as more of an antique shop than a junk shop and his prices tended to bear this out, but Baxter knew that he was far more likely to turn up something interesting at Monty's place than most of the others, even if he was less likely to be able to afford what he found.

Baxter was right at the back of some dimly lit room, trying to squeeze between a fancy lamp-stand and a table piled high with crockery, and Monty was over by the counter reading his paper when Baxter noticed an old mahogany box, about the same size as a small medicine cabinet. He eased it out from under an encyclopedia. The box was surprisingly heavy, which gave Baxter hope that it might contain something particularly old or unusual. He set it down on a rickety old table, pushed back its little latches and carefully opened the lid.

A powerful smell of mildew came up from the plush interior as Baxter caught his first glimpse of a gleaming set of silver instruments – tiny knives, needles and pairs of pincers – all laid out on a bed of velvet and each in their own custom-made cavity. Two corked phials were strapped into the box's lid, along with some sort of eyepiece and a well-thumbed manual. It looked like a set of tools which might have belonged to a dentist or a watchmaker.

'What's this?' Baxter called out to Monty.

Monty looked up, put down his newspaper and strolled over to see what Baxter had found.

'Ah now, *those*', he announced with some relish, 'are a lepidoctor's surgical implements.' He picked out a particularly deadly looking blade and studied it. 'Late Victorian. Very rare. I've not had a set of that sort of quality for nigh on thirty years.'

Baxter picked out a pair of tweezers. They were beautifully constructed but finely fringed with rust. 'A lepi*what*?' he said.

'A *lepidoctor*,' Monty told him. 'Bit of a lost art these days. And probably something of a secret society way back then.'

Baxter replaced the rusty tweezers and brushed his fingers over the other instruments. 'Yes,' he said, 'but what are they *for*?'

Monty shook his head, as if despairing at the depths to which educational standards had fallen. 'A lepidoctor', he said, 'was someone who specialized in carrying out repairs to butterflies.'

If you had asked Baxter Campbell at that particular moment if he properly appreciated the significance of his discovery and whether he recalled the peculiar exhibition from a fortnight before he may not have been able to tell you. All he knew was that he wanted to *own* that box of tricks more than he'd ever wanted to own anything. He had fallen in love with its strange array of sinister instruments long before he understood what purpose they served. All the same, Baxter had spent enough time in the company of second-hand dealers to know that it never pays to show your enthusiasm. So he continued to quietly pick over the silver implements. He slipped the magnifying glass out of its leather strap – the sort of eyepiece jewellers use to examine diamonds – and blew the dust off it. He put it up to his eye: it was a perfect fit.

'So, what's it worth?' he said, as he leant forward and examined the other tools through it.

'Well, that depends', said Monty Eldridge slyly, 'on what someone's willing to pay.'

It took quite a while to get old Monty to say how much he wanted for the lepidoctor's instruments and, almost inevitably, it was far more money than Baxter could hope to find. But Monty happened to remember an old gramophone Baxter had bought off him a year or two earlier (whilst explicitly failing to mention the fellow who'd been offering good money to get his hands on one) and it took another five minutes' hard bargaining before a deal was struck, in which Baxter agreed to trade in his old gramophone and fix the gears and brakes on Monty's bicycle in return for that box of surgical tools.

When Baxter finally took the mahogany box home a few days later he whisked it straight up to his room and closed the door behind him. This was, in itself, highly unusual. His father was normally the first person to whom he'd show some new, peculiar find. He placed the box on his bed and knelt down beside it. He opened it up and took out each silver tool in turn. He examined them all through the dusty eyepiece. None appeared to be broken, although he thought the spring on a pair of pincers would probably benefit from being replaced. The two glass jars were empty, or, at least, what little remained in them had set solid, like old varnish. Baxter pulled out the booklet and had a quick flick through it. The binding was split and the pages were worn and grubby, as if the previous owner must have thumbed through it a thousand times.

He turned to the first page and started reading. In the third paragraph he read:

> There is no reason to suppose that any moth or butterfly should be entirely beyond resuscitation, no matter how many weeks or months they have lain inert, as long as the internal organs are present and correct or may be easily rectified and the wings, antennae, etc. are not too badly decayed.

Baxter felt his heartbeat quicken – could feel it pumping in his ears. If there had been any lingering doubts as to what he must do, they promptly evaporated. In anyone's life there are few enough occasions when one is absolutely certain of something: when the facts stand right before you like some solid, unmovable truth. But Baxter knew, as he sat there with the room slowly darkening about him, that this was one such occasion and that his course of action was laid out for him.

Over the next couple of days he worked through the worn-out manual from cover to cover, then went back to the start and read through it again. Some of the words were distinctly old-fashioned and he had to look up quite a few in the huge old dictionary he'd picked up in a charity shop six months before. Fortunately, the manual contained its own short glossary, where most of the technical phrases of butterfly repair were explained and by the time he'd read right through it a third, then a fourth time Baxter found that the instructions had begun to make their own strange sense.

The book described six quite complicated procedures which, the reader was assured, would take care of the vast majority of butterfly injuries. Baxter was fairly mechanically minded, which is to say that he had repaired several dozen bicycles and replaced valves and soldered loose connections in as many wirelesses. But he couldn't help but feel that tinkering with the wings or the insides of such a delicate creature was an altogether different proposition to replacing a spring on a radio dial.

He cleaned all the tools with wire wool and methylated spirits and, by following the diagrams, acted out the intricate operations on imaginary butterflies, to the point where he just about managed to convince himself that he might have a hope of pulling it off. The problem was that at least half the operations contained the instruction 'Apply sealing gum' and every procedure concluded with the instruction to 'administer revivifying fluid'. Applying the sealing gum seemed remarkably similar to applying glue to paper. Administering revivifying fluid seemed to consist of nothing more than pulling the cork from one of the bottles quite close to the butterfly, and watching it spring back into life. However, the jars which had once contained the 'sealing gum' and 'revivifying fluid' were both practically empty. If any butterflies were to be revived Baxter would have to get his hands on the necessary gums and fluids. Until this had been done there was no point even contemplating how to get the butterflies out of the museum and up into his room.

'Lepidoctors' didn't feature at all in the local telephone directory and there was no sign of them in his big old dictionary. Baxter concluded that either the word was so incredibly old that it had fallen out of circulation or was so shrouded in secrecy that even the most formidable-looking books didn't dare whisper its name.

He had just about given up hope of ever finding the appropriate glues and fluids when he made a timely discovery. He was tugging at the leather strap which held the bottles in the lid when the silken upholstery came away in his hand. There, beneath it, on the bare wood was a printed label, which read 'Lepidoctors' supplies c/o Watkins and Donalds, 119, Hartley Road, London W11.'

Baxter knew he had an old London street map somewhere but, like a lot of things, it took a while to find it. He finally tracked it down up in the attic in a stack of 1950s wrestling magazines. Baxter opened out the map on his bedroom floor and in a matter of minutes managed to establish that Hartley Road was somewhere between Westbourne Grove and Portobello Road. So, on the following Saturday, instead of doing his usual round of museums, second-hand shops and jumble sales, he took the train to London's Paddington Station and, with his old map of London flapping about before him, followed the maze of streets to what he hoped would be the main supplier to the country's remaining lepidoctors.

Hartley Road itself was decidedly ordinary, with a terrace of houses down one side and a couple of blocks of flats on the other. Right from the start it didn't quite feel like the kind of place where a boy might get his hands on butterfly remedies. As he walked along, Baxter kept an eye on the house numbers and soon noticed a row of four or five shops up ahead. When he finally stood before them his heart sank. There was a pub, a newsagent, a launderette and a chemist. The same row of shops you'd expect to find in any town. There were no shadowy doorways, as Baxter had hoped for – no intercoms into which he could conduct some whispered conversation. Nothing secretive or sinister at all.

Number 119 was the chemist's shop. The numbers were stencilled in gold on to the glass above the doorway. The shop window was filled with a display of boxes of hair dye. On each packet a middle-aged man with dark brown or jet-black hair smiled out at the world. This in itself was a bit of an eye-opener. Baxter was vaguely aware that some women dyed their hair, but had no idea that men were at it. It was news, but not exactly big news. Yet, Baxter had a sneaking suspicion that this might be about as exciting a revelation as he was likely to have that day.

All the same, he was not about to go home without at least making a cursory enquiry, so he pushed the door, which set a small bell ringing above it, and by the time he got to the counter an Indian man in his fifties or sixties had emerged from behind a curtain and was there to meet him. He was a kind-looking fellow – quite thin, with a head full of wavy, grey hair. It occurred to Baxter that, with so many boxes of men's hair dye in his shop window, the proprietor might have considered dyeing his own hair. The only reason Baxter could come up with for him *not* dyeing it was that he might actually *like* it grey.

'How can I help you?' the chemist asked Baxter.

Baxter was finding it hard to concentrate. He kept thinking about grey hair and why someone may or may not want to dye it. He glanced up at the shelves to his left and right, as if he might find a sign for 'Butterfly Gum' or 'Revivifying Fluid', but there was nothing but toothpaste and aspirin and flu remedies, just like in any regular chemists.

Without quite knowing why, Baxter placed his hands on the counter before him – perhaps to try and stop himself from collapsing in a faint. He leant forward, which encouraged the chemist to do the same.

'I need some *supplies*,' Baxter whispered.

The chemist didn't move a muscle. 'And what sort of *supplies* exactly are we talking about?' he whispered in reply.

Baxter leant even further forward, so that his mouth was right up to the ear of the chemist, which was tucked away among all that wavy, grey hair.

'A *lepidoctor's* supplies,' said Baxter.

The chemist stood up straight and stared back down at Baxter as if he was completely bonkers. Baxter searched the chemist's face for some hint of comprehension, but found nothing. In fact, the fellow looked as if he was considering calling the police. Baxter was ready to give up, but thought that as he had come all this way and had made such a fool of himself already he had nothing to lose but the last few shreds of his dignity. He reached into his jacket pockets and pulled out the two empty phials from his lepidoctor's kit. He held them up, where there could be no mistaking them. The chemist stared at one jar, then the other. He glanced at the door over Baxter's shoulder, pulled back the curtain and nodded his head towards it.

'In here,' he said.

The room was not much bigger than a pantry. The

shelves on all four walls were packed with great tubs of pills and boxes of sticking plasters. Without saying a word the chemist headed over to an old wooden cupboard. He took a tiny key from his jacket pocket, unlocked it and opened the doors to reveal a whole, lost world of lotions and potions and ancient remedies. Half the jars seemed to contain bits of bark or dried herbs. The rest were filled with exotic-coloured oils. The chemist took Baxter's phials from him, looked them over and set them down on a wooden worktop.

'How much do you need?' the chemist asked him.

Baxter hadn't the faintest idea.

'Put it this way,' said the chemist, helpfully. 'How many butterflies are you hoping to repair?'

Baxter was a little taken aback to be talking so openly on the subject. He tried to picture the huge mosaic on the wall of the museum. He shrugged his shoulders. 'Maybe a thousand,' he said.

The chemist raised his eyebrows and let out a low whistle, apparently quite impressed with Baxter's plans. Then he turned back to his cupboard and lifted down a large jar of something syrupy and placed it on the counter. He unscrewed the lid and began to ladle the contents into a smaller bottle – about the size of a jam jar.

'If you don't mind me asking,' said the chemist as he continued ladling, 'where did you happen to come across the implements?'

'A junk shop,' Baxter told him and imagined Monty's horror at such a description.

'That's quite a find,' said the chemist and screwed the lid down tight on the jar. 'Do you know what you're doing?'

For some reason, the question cut right through Baxter's defences, and suddenly all his anxieties about repairing the butterflies, which he'd done his best to bury, began to shift and turn inside him. 'Not entirely, no,' he said, at last.

'You'll be fine,' the chemist told him. 'Just stick to the manual. And don't use too much glue.'

He returned to his old cupboard and took down a large brown bottle, which he seemed to handle with a good deal more care than the previous one. He turned his head away as he prepared to remove the large cork which plugged the top of the bottle, then suddenly stopped.

'Now, this revivifying fluid,' he said, and faltered slightly. 'You know, it's not exactly cheap.'

Baxter had to admit that he didn't. 'What's it going to cost me?' he said.

'The sort of numbers you've got in mind . . .' said the chemist and did a bit of quick mental arithmetic, 'you're talking about a hundred and fifty quid.'

Baxter felt his jaw drop. There was no way in the world he could conjure up that kind of money. He'd just begun to feel a little confidence growing in him. Now all his hopes were dashed again.

The grey-haired chemist could clearly see what Baxter was thinking.

'If that's a bit steep,' he said, 'there is an alternative.'

Baxter said he'd like to hear it.

'Menthol,' the chemist told him.

Baxter was none the wiser.

'Just suck on a cough sweet for a couple of minutes,' the chemist explained. 'Then exhale.'

He pursed his lips and gently breathed out into the palm of his hand.

'Does it work?' said Baxter.

The chemist nodded at him. 'Oh yes,' he said.

The old man popped his head back through the curtain to make sure that no one was watching, then ushered Baxter back into the shop. He took a handful of packets of cough sweets down from the shelf and packed them into a brown paper bag, along with the jar of adhesive, then totted everything up on his till.

The whole lot came to less than a fiver. Back behind his counter, the old man looked like an ordinary chemist again. Baxter paid, picked up his bag, thanked the chemist and headed for the door. He'd almost reached it when he stopped and turned.

'Do you mind if I ask you a question?' he said.

The chemist shook his head. 'Fire away,' he said.

Baxter was having trouble putting his thoughts into words. 'If you've . . . If you've never actually *done* it before,' he said, 'how do you know if you're doing it properly?'

The chemist thought about it for a moment. 'It's the same as anything else,' he said eventually. 'You just pick it up as you go along.'

The actual break-in took less than a week's preparation. Baxter visited the museum on two separate occasions, discreetly investigating its every nook and cranny, then back in his bedroom, drew up plans of the layout of the building, devised a route through it and compiled a list of exactly which part of the museum he hoped to be in at what particular time.

His biggest concern was how to transport the butterflies. He'd never actually handled one, but it was perfectly clear that if they got knocked about too much between the museum and his bedroom there wouldn't be much hope of them being brought back to life. His first thought was to use his old cricket bag. Then he began to favour the sheet off his bed with all the butterflies gathered up in the middle. But he finally settled on a canvas rucksack he'd bought at a jumble sale the previous summer. He reckoned it was probably big enough to accommodate all the butterflies and was less likely to attract any unwanted attention out on the street. The small brown envelopes were something of an afterthought. He'd bought a giant box of them from a closing down sale in a stationery shop in January and just had a hunch that they would come in handy one day.

On the Friday he raced home from school in under five minutes, picked up the rucksack he'd packed the night before and left a note for his father saying that he'd gone for a walk out to the rubbish dump and that he'd be back in a couple of hours. He got to the museum half an hour before closing and spent five minutes simply strolling around the place, in order to blend in with the other visitors. Then he slipped into the Gents and, once he'd satisfied himself that all the cubicles were empty, opened the broom cupboard he'd discovered on one of his earlier visits and quietly crept inside.

As far as he could tell the cupboard had been abandoned several years earlier. Baxter had taken pity on it and as he crouched on its floor clutching his rucksack he thought he sensed the cupboard's appreciation in being used again. At five o'clock, right on cue, someone popped their head into the Gents, called out, 'Anybody in?' turned the lights out and departed, leaving the door to slowly close on its spring. Baxter didn't move for another twenty minutes. He just sat in the dark and went through his itinerary one last time. At some point he ate a bar of chocolate, to keep his strength up. Then he crawled out, like some animal emerging from hibernation, and waited patiently by the wash basins for another twenty minutes, just as he had planned to do.

He picked up his rucksack, put his head out into the museum and listened. He couldn't hear a thing. Then he tiptoed out into the darkened gallery and began to make his way down one of the aisles. The whole museum felt very different in the half-light. Everything was vague and unfamiliar, as if the glass cabinets might house an entirely different collection of beast and artifact to those on show during the day.

Half-way down the aisle he stopped and pulled out the old miner's helmet he'd picked up at Monty's a couple of years earlier and sometimes used to read in bed. It had a torch fixed to the front, just above the peak. He had one final, good long listen. 'Hello?' he called out into the dark. Nobody answered. He waited another couple of moments, then turned the torch on his helmet on.

The glass case before him was suddenly illuminated. Inside, a pair of owls sat and stared at him, rather haughtily. Baxter did his best to ignore them and as he went on his way the owls' shadows slowly shifted, until they settled back into the dark.

Every worn old bone and bit of broken pottery seemed to be aware of his presence and somewhat alarmed that anyone should be creeping around the place after dark. Baxter avoided looking into the cabinet which contained the handcuffs. He didn't want to consider the consequences of being caught.

When he finally stepped into the large white room the

light from the lamp on his helmet suddenly spread and filled the place, as if he was a pot-holer who'd just come out into some underground cavern. The giant butterfly was still there – still pinned in position. Baxter tiptoed over to it. He put his face right up to one of the butterflies. Its fine black wings were laced with blue and gold.

'Let's see what we can do for you,' he said.

It took him a while to work out how to remove the pins without causing even more damage, but found that by sliding the nails of his thumb and middle finger under the head of each pin and giving it a sharp tug, both the pin and the butterfly came quite cleanly away from the wall. Then it was just a moment's work to take the butterfly off its skewer and slip it into its own little envelope. He studied the first three or four. All were punctured by the tiniest holes. And as he carried on he wondered, not for the first time, if it really would prove to be possible to revive a creature that had effectively been crucified.

After half an hour the sheer effort of concentration was beginning to make Baxter's head spin. After an hour the tips of his fingers were dreadfully sore. By then he'd managed to prise away and deposit in their individual envelopes at least two-thirds of the butterflies. The rest were out of reach. So Baxter set off to try and find something to stand on.

He walked around the whole museum in his miner's helmet without finding a single chair or stool. In fact, the

only thing which looked as if it might be capable of
supporting him was the old polar bear. He dragged it back
and pushed its plinth right up against the gallery wall. It
was about the right height and when Baxter climbed up on
to its shoulders the bear's raised paws felt as if they were
holding on to his shins to stop him falling, which gave him
some much-needed confidence.

Half an hour later Baxter slipped the last butterfly into
its brown envelope. All that remained were a thousand tiny
holes in the wall in the shape of a butterfly, and a thousand
pins scattered about the floor. The polar bear leant against
the wall, apparently exhausted. When the head of the
museum arrived the following morning it would look
suspiciously like the polar bear had dragged itself into the
snow-white gallery where it had indulged in a midnight
feast of butterflies. Whatever had taken place the polar
bear had clearly played some part in it, but the bear, like
every other animal in the museum, was keeping mum.

Baxter slipped out on to the street and pulled the
museum door to behind him. His rucksack was full, but
not too heavy. Those precious envelopes made him walk
with a great deal of care. He saw himself as some sort of
Postman of the Butterflies. He walked with his head up, so
as not to look guilty, and everything went smoothly until
he was less than a hundred yards from his house and he
bumped into Mister Matlock, one of the neighbours, who
happened to be out walking his dog.

'Hello, young Baxter,' he said. 'Have you been camping?'

Baxter didn't much like Mister Matlock. He was the sort of person who was always smiling but never seemed to be thinking particularly nice thoughts.

'It's a new rucksack,' Baxter said. 'So I thought I'd give it a try-out. You know, just a couple of times round the block.'

Mister Matlock smiled but his eyes were as dead as a dodo's. It was always his eyes that gave him away – as if he was thinking that if he had *his* way, Baxter's house would be bulldozed and he and his dad thrown out of town.

Baxter said goodnight, pressed on and as soon as he was in the house, crept up to his room and locked the door. He undid the rucksack's drawstring, gently upended it and watched as a thousand envelopes spilled on to the bed. Baxter thought it was probably about as close to flying the butterflies had got since that terrible moment when they found themselves in Milton Spufford's killing jar. It was now up to him to see if he could get them flying again.

He pulled out his box of tools from under the bed and set it down on his old desk. He adjusted the height of his stool, turned the lamp on, reached over to his bed and picked an envelope off the top of the pile. He put the magnifying glass up to his eye and held it there like a monocle. Then he set to work.

There was a tiny hole where the pin had been inserted and on the other side of the butterfly, where the pin had surfaced, a minuscule tear. This allowed Baxter to peel back the skin with his tweezers and to have a look inside without making any extra incisions. As far as he could tell, most of the muscle and tissue was intact and, according to the manual, all that was necessary was to carefully knit the flesh back together, apply a drop of gum and revivify.

That first butterfly was a stunning combination of black and amber, with unusually frilly wings. Baxter carefully repaired it, glued it and let it dry for several minutes before daring to attempt to revive it. Then, when he felt quite sure that the adhesive had set, he unwrapped his first cough sweet and slipped it into his mouth. He sucked away until he could taste all the medicinal flavours seep into his tongue and felt his nose begin to tingle. He placed the butterfly in the palm of his hand, just like the chemist had shown him. He rubbed the cough sweet up against the roof of his mouth a couple of times and with the butterfly no more than six inches from him, gently breathed his warm, mentholy breath over it.

For a moment or two nothing happened. The butterfly just sat there, as mute and motionless as it had been on the museum wall. Baxter felt a great wave of disappointment rise up in him and he was about to give the butterfly a second dose when its wings suddenly twitched. It flexed its tiny antennae and moved its six little legs. And the whole elegant creature began to slowly stretch and shift in Baxter's hand.

Baxter laughed out loud as he stared at what had been, until a few minutes earlier, a beautiful but lifeless thing. And yet he was simply witnessing what he'd endlessly dreamt of – of breathing life back into a butterfly. Within ten minutes he had successfully repaired another half-dozen, which were all happily fluttering about his room. Baxter was overjoyed but soon realized that this arrangement was far from practical, so he caught each one in his cupped hands, climbed the steps in the corner up to the attic and from then on, as soon as each one showed the first signs of life he would gather it up and release it through the trapdoor into the attic where it joined all the other revitalized butterflies.

He worked right through the night, with that magnifying glass up to his eye as he delicately nipped and sealed and knitted. Now and then an envelope would contain a butterfly with more serious internal damage and Baxter would have to consult his manual and employ some of the more unusual surgical tools. But by the morning he had revived what he estimated to be about three hundred butterflies and decided he had better go downstairs for some breakfast, if only to revive himself.

Half an hour later he was back at his operating table. By mid-morning he had sucked his way through all five packets of cough sweets and had to slip out to the newsagents and buy another dozen or so. The woman behind the counter told him, 'If your cough's that bad you should maybe see a doctor.' But Baxter said he just liked the taste of them, which, by this stage, wasn't entirely true.

For the rest of the day he worked almost without stopping. Every couple of hours he would have a little walk around the room, just to stretch his arms and legs. Each time he did so he noticed how the pile of envelopes on his bedspread had grown a little smaller. And every time he looked out of his window he saw how the sun had moved a little further through the sky.

The biggest upset occurred after he'd fixed the wings on a particularly large specimen, which were a luminous turquoise, like a peacock's. He blew some menthol over it, but the moment it sputtered back into being it became clear that one of its wings was still not quite right. Baxter had to carry out further repairs with it flapping and twitching between his fingers. Once he'd managed to complete all his sewing and gluing, the creature seemed perfectly happy but it was a most unpleasant experience and Baxter vowed that from that point forward he would refrain from reviving a butterfly until he was absolutely certain that all the work was done.

At about six or seven on the Saturday evening he went down for his dinner, but was so excited by how few envelopes remained unopened that he was determined to get back to them as soon as possible. In those last few hours he began to have problems with his eyesight. His vision became quite blurred and he could feel a terrible headache coming on. And by the time he had repaired and revived the last one and released it into the attic it was long past midnight. He felt as if he'd run a marathon. He lay on his bed and calculated that he must have sucked his way through at least two hundred cough sweets. He wondered if he would ever get the taste of them out of his mouth. He closed his eyes. He just needed to close them for a second. And within a minute he was fast asleep.

He awoke with a jolt about four hours later. The sun was rising. He looked at his watch. Almost six o'clock. He sat himself up and when he was sure that he was awake and had got his thoughts in order he went over to the corner of the bedroom and quietly climbed the wooden steps.

He opened the trapdoor, very gently, expecting to find the attic full of frantic life, but the room was perfectly still. He climbed the last few steps and closed the trapdoor behind him. And as he stood there he was suddenly gripped by the fear that all his butterflies had flown away before he'd had the chance to see them together, or had slipped back into their slumber after only a few snatched hours of life. But as his eyes slowly grew accustomed to the darkness, he began to see them – a coat of butterflies covering all his old tape recorders and broken radios, their wings slowly winding backwards and forwards, as if they'd been waiting for him.

He carefully made his way over to the skylight and
pushed it open. Then he slowly crept back to the far side
of the room. For a minute the attic was still again. There
was just the sound of the town slowly waking far below
him and Baxter up in his attic among his butterflies. The
sun continued to rise above the rooftops and a gentle
breeze swept in through the skylight. The butterflies
began to stir. The first few took to the air and fluttered
about the rafters. The others gradually joined them on the
wing. And soon the air was full of butterflies – every
colour and every design – until one or two danced out of
the skylight, the others followed and in an instant all that
delicate life swept out of the room.

Baxter went over to the open skylight and watched them
leaving: a great cloud of butterflies rolling over the town.
They seemed to know where they were going. They
seemed to know what they had to do.

Later that same day Milton Spufford, artist and butterfly
collector, was standing up on the Downs, with the Weald
to the north and the sea to the south and nothing but open
hillside all around him, when he spotted an interesting-
looking butterfly about ten feet away.

It was his first find of the day. In his right hand he held
his butterfly net by the handle. In his left he gripped his
killing jar. His eyes never left his prey as he crept over
towards it. Its wings were pale green, like two young

leaves, and Milton was already imagining what it would look like with all the life drawn out of it and pinned to a museum wall. He got within striking distance and for a moment watched the creature feeding. He raised his net – the same net that had already imprisoned a thousand other butterflies.

'You're coming home with *me*,' he whispered.

He was about to bring his net down when a dark shadow swept silently over him. The temperature suddenly dropped. The sun was gone and Milton turned to find the silhouette of a massive butterfly hovering above him. The same one he'd so meticulously constructed from a thousand stifled butterflies.

He dropped the net. His killing jar went rolling down the hillside. The giant butterfly slowly flapped its wings. And as he stood there, gaping at his own strange creation, the huge butterfly fell upon him and wrapped itself around him, until Milton Spufford all but disappeared.

He mustn't have struggled for much more than a minute. With his last breath he tried to call out, but his words were muffled by the butterflies as they gently smothered him. For those last few moments he was full of colour. He was alive among his butterflies. Until the butterfly collector was finally extinguished and his lifeless body fell to the ground.

He lay on the grass, as if he was deeply sleeping. And when an old lady came across him not long after, she found nothing remotely suspicious in the circumstances. It was a beautiful day, she told the inquest, with the sun high in the sky, a gentle wind blowing and hundreds of butterflies dancing everywhere.

Hermit wanted

Some people are born rich. Some become rich. Others aren't quite so fortunate. Giles and Virginia Jarvis were of the fortunate variety. Giles had made lots of money working in the City. Ginny had inherited hers from her mum and dad. So when they married it was like a great clanging-together of bank vaults that rang out across the land.

They bought a big old house out in the country with dozens of bedrooms and stone columns at either side of the front door and a long gravel drive which swept up to it through the hundreds of acres of woodland that came with the estate. They liked the idea of running their house in the way a squire and his wife might have run it a couple of centuries earlier, so they created a deer park and commissioned a couple of follies and a croquet lawn with peacocks strutting around it, and employed plenty of staff to do all the cooking and cleaning and to treat Giles and Ginny with the kind of respect they felt their considerable wealth deserved.

One Saturday morning Ginny was riding her horse through a part of the woods she'd never explored before when she happened to come across a dank little cave. She climbed off her horse, crept up to the entrance and peered into the darkness.

'Hello?' she said.

A minute later she was back on her horse and charging towards the house, barely able to contain her excitement. She abandoned her horse at the front door and went haring straight up the stairs in her muddy boots.

'*Giles*,' she called out, 'Giles, *darling*,' and her words went flapping all around the high ceiling and echoing up and down the corridors.

Her husband peered over a banister, convinced that Ginny had done something truly dreadful, like take a pot-shot at some pesky pigeon and hit a local by mistake. But when he finally located his wife she was positively beaming.

'I've found a *cave*,' she said.

It wasn't the sort of news that Giles had expected and it took him a couple of moments to come up with what felt like an appropriate response.

'Well done,' he said, at last.

'We must get ourselves a *hermit* for it,' Ginny declared. 'Like people used to.'

Unlike his wife, Giles had never paid much attention in history lessons and consequently wasn't up on hermits and, more precisely, what a hermit was *for*. But, as Ginny explained that afternoon and all through supper, one doesn't have a hermit *for* anything in particular, except for looking rather wild and living a life of solitude and generally occupying what would otherwise be an empty cave.

At first, Giles found the idea rather baffling. But within a couple of days he began to think it quite a novelty. And by the end of the week he considered a hermit an absolute necessity and was quite indignant that no one had brought it to his attention earlier on.

The following week they put an advert in the local newspaper, under Situations Vacant:

HERMIT WANTED
Free meals and accommodation.
Situated on grand estate.
Would suit the quiet type.

with their name and address printed beneath it, to which all aspiring hermits should apply.

The Jarvises had high hopes. After all, they reasoned, how many jobs could there be which offered free meals and accommodation for doing nothing except sitting and thinking all day? So they were, frankly, surprised and a little disappointed when, a full week later, they hadn't received a single application. How very strange, they thought. Then, how very *ungrateful*. Here they were, offering a cave with all the trimmings and the general public were too hoity-toity to take them up on it.

Ginny began to talk vaguely about turning the cave into

a grotto and making up a couple of sightings of fairies, to stimulate interest. Either that or just filling the damned thing in. But the following Tuesday as they took tea in one of their many lounges and listened to a concert on the radio a maid shuffled in and announced that a rather rough-looking fellow had fetched up at the back door and was asking if the hermit job was still available.

Ginny let out a little yelp – a peculiar noise, similar to a small dog being trodden on, which, in Ginny, tended to indicate profound delight. Giles hadn't heard that little yelp half as much as he would've liked to lately so, to show his support, he slapped his thigh and let out a low guffaw of his own.

The maid was told to take the fellow through to the library and, a couple of minutes later, Ginny and Giles strolled in after him. He was an oldish chap – in his fifties or sixties – and was standing before the shelves of books looking thoroughly dumbfounded, as if he'd been thrown into a book-prison.

'Do you read much?' Ginny asked, by way of starting up a conversation.

The fellow turned and shrugged, as if he didn't have particularly strong feelings on the subject either way.

'I *know*,' said Ginny, 'it's so hard to find the time.'

As she spoke, Ginny gave her budding hermit a quick once-over. He was a fairly bedraggled specimen, which was no bad thing since bedragglement was quite fitting for a hermit, but there was a ripe old smell about the fellow so, rather than risk him ruining their upholstered furniture, Ginny found him a wooden chair to sit on, thinking it might be easier to have it scrubbed clean after he'd departed. Or burned, if necessary.

Giles and Ginny settled themselves on to one of the enormous sofas and for a moment simply sat and observed their guest as he continued to marvel at the opulence of his surroundings.

'Are you a religious man?' Ginny asked, eventually.

The fellow considered the question, then shrugged. 'Not really,' he said.

Ginny could see that her guest wasn't particularly well versed in the art of chit-chat. 'But, if you don't mind me saying,' she said, 'you strike me as someone who likes to do a little *thinking*.'

The fellow thought about it for a moment. 'I suppose,' he said, then nodded. 'Yes, I sometimes like to *think*.'

Ginny smiled, as if the fellow was finally confirming the sort of intelligence she had suspected him of having, and she took this as a cue to go more fully into what the job entailed. They had a cave, she explained, and wanted someone to live in it. Someone who might cultivate the long-haired, solitary attitude of a hermit.

As she spoke the bedraggled fellow nodded but continued to gaze around the room.

'Which means that you must agree not to shave, or cut

79

your hair, or trim your fingernails,' Ginny insisted. 'We want that *savage* look.'

The fellow nodded again.

'And you must stay in your cave – or thereabouts,' Giles added, in case there was any chance the fellow had failed to grasp the whole living-in-a-cave idea.

The fellow nodded once more, then all three of them sat in silence for a moment, until the old fellow suddenly seemed to find his voice.

'There was something about food . . .' he said, '. . . in the advert.'

'That's right,' said Ginny. 'One of the staff will drop something off every morning. You know, a little bread and cheese – that sort of thing.'

This talk of bread and cheese certainly seemed to perk the old fellow up and, not long after, he suddenly sprang to his feet, like some soldier standing to attention.

'Right then,' he said.

'Very good,' said Ginny, and she and Giles hauled themselves up from their sofa. 'When would you be able to start?'

The old fellow tugged back his jacket sleeve and stared at his wrist, as if a watch might suddenly appear there.

'Well, straightaway,' he said.

So they all marched down to the cloakroom, where Giles and Ginny pulled on their wellington boots. Then they all trooped out through the back door and headed off towards the woods. As they marched along Ginny did her

best to impress upon her newly appointed hermit what
sort of behaviour was expected of him. Contemplation, she
said. That was what they were after. Nothing too noisy or
demonstrative.

'As a rule, hermits tend to be quite introverted,' she told
him.

Ginny had envisaged her hermit dressed in a shroud or
simple cassock, but the old fellow's clothes were already so
rough and ragged that she saw no need to make a fuss.
Enquiries were made as to whether there were family
members who might need to be informed of his new
position or any personal knick-knacks which might need
picking up. There weren't.

'We'll have one of the boys bring you out an old straw
mattress,' Ginny told him as they continued walking. 'And
a spade,' she said, and waved vaguely at the woods off to
her right, 'for your convenience.'

They finally reached the cave and the hermit stared into
it without much enthusiasm. Giles and Ginny worried he
might be about to turn and walk away. But he shrugged, as
he seemed to be in the habit of doing, and said that he'd
seen worse. Then Ginny told him about the vow of silence,
which she said she hoped that he would agree to.

'Silence?' said the hermit.

Ginny nodded. 'Most hermits appreciate a little peace
and quiet,' she told him. 'It helps them *think*.'

The hermit gave another shrug, which Ginny took as

his consent on the issue. 'Oh, and if anything interesting occurs to you while you're thinking,' she said, 'you must feel free to share your thoughts with us.'

The hermit looked stumped. 'How do I tell you what I'm thinking if I'm not allowed to talk?' he said.

'We'll have some paper and pencils sent over,' Ginny told him. 'Just jot down any thoughts and leave them at the cave entrance. One of the staff will pick them up.'

They stood around for another few moments. Then Giles announced that he believed that they had taken care of everything and he and Ginny were about to leave when the hermit raised his hand, like a schoolboy.

'About the bread and cheese,' he said.

'Of course,' said Ginny. 'We'll send it over with the mattress.' Then she brought her finger up to her mouth, as if that simple gesture effectively stifled every last word he might otherwise have uttered in his insignificant little life.

'Remember,' she said, 'as quiet as the grave.'

For the first couple of months the Jarvises were quite besotted with their hermit and would use any excuse to drop in on him. His hair had been quite lank and greasy to begin with, but as it grew, along with his beard and fingernails, he looked more like the wild man Ginny and Giles had imagined and became ever more popular with them. At dinner parties they would talk with great affection of their 'noble savage' and sometimes gather together great packs of guests to creep up to the cave and spy on him as he went about his contemplative chores.

For his part, the hermit was reasonably happy with the arrangements – at least to begin with. He had somewhere to sleep, even if it was quite damp and draughty. More importantly, he had a regular supply of food delivered to his front door. A plate of sandwiches would appear outside his cave first thing in the morning along with fresh fruit and the occasional buttered scone. But as the months crept by the quality of food gradually deteriorated. One day there was nothing but a bag of rotten apples waiting for him. A pot of mouldy old broth turned up the following week. Then he began to be given what looked suspiciously like the scraps from the Jarvis's previous night's dinner. And some days there would be no food at all.

But it was the silence that did the damage. The hermit had never been one for inconsequential conversation and, in fairness, there had been the odd day when he quite enjoyed the solitude. But his vow of silence soon became a burden. It hung around him like heavy chains. And after several months spent staring out at the dismal weather or huddled under his blanket against the cave's cold wall he found his thoughts beginning to take unusual routes and strange diversions and his mind begin to unravel as it went along.

Giles and Ginny, meanwhile, had found a new distraction. Giles was dozing by the fire one night when his wife sat down and snuggled up beside him.

'I've got some news,' she said.

'What's up?' said Giles.

'Come summer,' she said, 'I wouldn't be at all surprised if there wasn't a new little junior Jarvis pottering about the place.' And she made that little yelp which her husband loved so much and heard so rarely. 'Daddy's going to have himself an heir to the throne,' she said.

The next few months were a frenzy of planning and preparation. Rooms had to be redecorated and converted into nurseries. Nannies and other help had to be interviewed and hired. Week by week, Ginny grew a little heavier and eventually became so exhausted that she spent most of the last month of her pregnancy laid up in her bedroom, before the midwife was finally called and duly delivered a baby boy named Jack who, if he only knew it, was bound for a life of suffocating wealth.

At that point any remaining interest in the wild old man in the woods promptly evaporated and all their attention was directed towards their son. Jack spent most of his days on his back, staring up at the ceiling until the face of a nanny or a mother or father peered in at him. He slept and fed; was changed and bathed. And late at night, in those moments before his mother reached him, his cries would carry through the nursery window – out into the darkness and deep into the woods.

The hermit's messages had started out quite innocently, with maids returning to the house with bits of paper

84

proclaiming

BETWEEN THE TREES ARE MORE TREES

and

A CAVE IS BUT AN OPEN MOUTH

But over the months they began to take on a more disturbed tone, with notes such as

TOO MANY INSECTS

and

THE DOG IS HOWLING IN MY HEAD

Some of his notes began to contain peculiar drawings; others were covered in illegible scrawl. But by then the Jarvises had grown quite bored, had told their staff not to bother them with his infernal rantings and had more or less washed their hands of him.

The first real sign of trouble was when the peacocks went missing. The maid who was sent out to try and round them up found their remains at the edge of the wood – two bloody carcasses among a few fancy feathers. It was a gruesome, if isolated, incident which sent a small shudder of fear right through the household. But there was no way of knowing exactly who or what was responsible. It could quite conceivably have been a fox. Over the next few days the hermit was seen wandering all over the grounds and acting most peculiar. With his long hair and long nails, he wasn't the kind of fellow the staff wished to stumble across without fair warning. And when Giles found a note tucked under his car's windscreen wiper which said simply

RED IN TOOTH AND CLAW

he decided he'd had enough and sent some of the lads out to try and track the hermit down.

He wasn't in his cave and there was no sign of him in the deer park, so the lads split up and went hiking off into the woods. An hour or two later one of them came running up the drive to report a sighting of the wild old man. Giles took down his shotgun, called all the men on the estate together and had his scout lead them into the woods to the spot where the hermit had last been seen. They spread out and swept up the hill. They followed the valley. Between them they had binoculars, food and water, as well as Giles's anger to drive them on, but after three or four hours of leaping streams and hacking a path through the undergrowth they had nothing to show for their efforts, except arms and legs which were badly scratched by bracken and feet which were numb with cold.

They were out near a ridge and Giles was about ready to call a halt to the proceedings when one of the boys waved to get his attention and pointed over to the west. The whole party froze and stared out towards the line of trees on the horizon. But there was nothing there. Just the bare trees silhouetted against the cold, grey sky. Then a figure suddenly sprang up and darted from one tree to another. A gasp went round the lads and Giles brought his gun up to his shoulder. He closed one eye and waited. And when the figure next slipped out into the open he let both barrels go.

Every bird in the woods took to the sky in a mad clatter of flapping and cawing. The gunshots rang out for miles around. For a while, nobody dared move a muscle.

'Do you think we hit him?' Giles asked the others.

The boy beside him was quite convinced he hadn't got within ten yards of him.

'I think you may have winged him, sir,' he said.

Then everyone ran up to the ridge where the figure was last seen moving. They looked hard but found no sign of him, nor any spots of blood.

'Well, that should've scared the mad old rogue back to wherever he came from,' Giles told the others. And, to a man, they all stood and nodded and agreed that it most definitely should.

It would be the last time Giles ever set eyes on the fellow. But for the rest of his days he would imagine himself back in the woods, bringing the gun up to his shoulder and doing a better job. For, two days later, when Jack's nanny slipped out of the nursery to warm a bottle, the window creaked open. And as little Jack lay on his back and stared up at the ceiling an unfamiliar face swung into view. He saw a matted beard and long, lank hair hanging

87

over him. He saw two hot, wild eyes look him up and down. And, at last, Jack saw a pair of hands with long, sharp fingernails reach down towards him – felt them slip beneath him and lift him up.

The nanny returned just in time to see the wild man ease himself out of the window, with the baby clutched to his shoulder. She screamed and, not long after, her mistress came running in to see what all the fuss was about. Ginny found the nanny still screaming and pointing towards the open window. She ran over to it. And the last thing she ever saw of her son was him looking back over the hermit's shoulder as he disappeared into the woods.

Of course, the police were called and the locals were alerted. Search parties were given descriptions and sent on their way. Vast rewards were offered for the baby's safe return or information which led to a satisfactory conclusion. And not surprisingly, the locals spent their every spare minute doing their best to claim the prize.

The Jarvises scoured the woods themselves but found no sign of the wild man. And, year by year, they came a little closer to accepting that they would never set eyes on their precious son again.

But from time to time there would be talk of a sighting – of some strange creature making his way through the undergrowth, clutching a youngster and, later, of the two of them running side by side. Five long years after they first disappeared, a local woman claimed to have come across two wild-looking creatures in a clearing near the edge of the estate and as soon as word got back to the house, she was summoned by Ginny Jarvis.

The woman stood in the library, looking quite intimidated, when the Jarvises walked in to meet her, just as they'd met the hermit all those years before. But Ginny insisted the woman sit on the sofa beside her and took her hand and told her to take her time and tell her all about the two figures she claimed to have seen.

The woman said that she'd only seen them for a matter of seconds before they noticed her and went scurrying back into the undergrowth.

'All I can say', she said, 'is that one was fully grown – an oldish fellow. And the other small, just like a child.'

Ginny begged her to go on.

'Both looked quite wild – with matted hair hanging round their shoulders,' the woman told her. 'And long, sharp fingernails.'

Ginny gripped the woman's hand in desperation and asked if there wasn't anything else she could tell her. 'Did either speak?' she asked.

'Not at all,' said the woman. 'They were both as silent as the grave.'

Alien abduction

Sitting at a desk all day can be very demanding. Pretending to look as if you're paying attention can be an almost impossible strain. The children of 4B were hot and tired and beginning to grow restless. And there were still twenty minutes to go before the bell was due to ring.

Theodore Gutch was watching the clock on the wall behind Mister Morgan – was watching the second hand slowly sweep around the clock's circumference until it finally found its way back up to the twelve.

'Twenty more of those,' thought Theodore, 'and I'll be a free man. Free to do whatever I please.'

Theodore looked around the room for something else to occupy him. He considered trying to hold his breath whilst counting the drawing pins on all four walls – a little trick he'd very nearly pulled off a couple of days earlier and may well have had another crack at it, had he not been distracted by a flash of light through the window to his left. Now, there is every chance that the flash of light was caused by someone on the other side of town opening a window. As that distant window shifted on its hinges it could have momentarily caught the sun. To be fair, even Theodore Gutch knew this to be the most likely explanation. But the previous week he'd read a book about an army of Martians landing in a small town in America and wreaking all sorts of havoc. And with nothing better to do with the remaining minutes of this particular Wednesday, it wasn't long before it occurred to him that the flash of light could just as easily have been the after-burners of some alien spacecraft as it landed in the playground in Lowerfold Park.

The threat of an alien invasion was certainly a lot more interesting than whatever Mister Morgan had to offer. Sometimes even Mister Morgan didn't seem especially interested in what he had to say. Theodore glanced around the room. Across the aisle, Robert Pinner was staring at the palm of his right hand, trying to work out from the lines which crossed it how long a life he had left to live.

Theodore plucked a piece of paper from one of his notebooks, picked up a pencil and scrawled a few words on it. 'A spaceship full of marshuns', he wrote (Theodore was not the best of spellers), 'has just landed in Lowerfold Park.'

Robert Pinner's ruminations were rudely interrupted when a paper plane landed on the desk right in front of him. It made him jump and he looked round to find Theodore Gutch staring back at him, as if his eyes were about to pop right out of his head.

Theodore nodded at the plane. 'Open it up,' he hissed.

Robert ducked his head down behind the boy sitting in front of him (a boy named Howie Barker who had plenty of body to hide behind) and carefully unfolded the piece of paper. He read the message, frowned and looked back at Theodore, who was now nodding his head most gravely.

'It's *true*,' he said, and did so with such conviction that Mister Morgan was obliged to stop in mid-sentence and ask Theodore if he might possibly refrain from talking when *he* was talking, as it rather interfered with his train of thought.

It doesn't take long for a rumour to do the rounds – especially a rumour concerning alien invasion – and there are few situations better suited to a rumour spreading than a room full of children who are bored to tears. Every time Mister Morgan turned his back there was a great flurry of activity, as Theodore's note and several new ones were frantically passed from desk to desk. One of the new notes stated, quite categorically, that '250 aliens' had landed. On another, Colin Benson had drawn the actual spaceship – a pointy rocket resting on two wide fins. Beside it he had attempted to draw his own idea of an actual alien, but couldn't get its head and arms quite right and in a fit of frustration had scribbled it out, which left the impression of a ghostly figure staring out through the interference on a TV screen.

With five minutes still to go before the bell, 4B was in a state of near-hysteria. Mandy Shaw thought she was going to wet herself with excitement. Barry Marsden gripped the edge of his desk so tightly that his knuckles had turned quite white. One or two children had taken the news quite badly. Others thought it was the most exciting thing to happen since the crisp factory went up in flames. A few pupils privately wondered whether the report was one hundred per cent accurate. But all were united in their determination to be on their feet as soon as the bell started ringing, to race round to the park and have a good look at this alien spacecraft for themselves.

Those last few minutes were fraught with tension. Mister Morgan could tell that there was something brewing: the whole classroom seemed to crackle with anticipation and everyone kept glancing over at the windows, as if they might catch sight of something unusual there.

'Perhaps there's going to be a fight,' thought Mister Morgan. Mister Morgan quite enjoyed a little fight. He liked striding in and taking charge of the situation. 'Break it up, break it up,' he'd say, as he dragged the two boys off each other. But there hadn't been a fight in the school playground for over a year and there was no point him asking the children what was going on. They never told him anything.

The moment the bell started ringing the children were out of their chairs and flying down the corridor. Every girl and boy they encountered was told all about the Martian invasion and every one of them instantly chose to join their ranks, until a great stampede of youth was rumbling down the steps and out into the daylight, carrying with it anyone not quick enough to get out of the way.

They piled into the park. They went roaring past the bowling green. They went hammering down the path between the empty tennis courts. They charged through the rose garden, all the way round the duck pond and under the rows of horse chestnuts, fully expecting to find some silver spaceship at the other end. Every child had their own idea of what that spacecraft was going to look like. Some imagined a colossal rocket with steam quietly pouring off it. Some fancied a great silver dish, parked up on the tarmac, with its ramp already down. Some expected to find aliens playing on the swings and round-about, but when they finally arrived at the playground the place was deserted – devoid not just of alien life, but any life at all.

The children slowly came to a standstill. For a while, an eerie silence filled the air. Then disappointment began to set in – the sort of disappointment that can easily turn into anger – until one of the younger children finally opened his mouth.

'Where'd they go?' he said.

The silence settled back over the crowd. Then another, older boy shouted, 'Someone's taken 'em!' And, just in case anyone hadn't understood what he meant the first time round, he added, 'Someone's abducted the aliens!'

A disgruntled murmur swept through the hordes of children. The names of various organizations that might conceivably kidnap aliens were bandied about, until a young girl, with no previous history of trouble-making, lifted both hands to her mouth and called out, 'Let's all go down to the Town Hall!'

It was a suggestion which was most warmly welcomed. The Town Hall seemed like exactly the right place to take their grievance and everyone had so enjoyed charging through the park like a herd of buffalo that they were keen to go charging off somewhere else.

So they all went roaring down the middle of Church Street. The grown-ups they passed had never seen the like. Cars had to pull up on to the pavement as the children ran cheering and screaming between them, and the owner of the sweet shop on the corner was so distraught at the sight of so many marauding youngsters that he decided to shut up shop and pulled down all the blinds.

Within five minutes the children arrived at the steps of the Town Hall and their defiant roar slowly subsided as it washed up against the hard grey walls of authority. Some of the children feared that their little adventure might now be over. They imagined themselves walking home, defeated and dejected. But the same young girl who'd rallied the troops back at the park brought her hands up to her mouth again.

'We *demand* to see the mayor!' she cried.

In no time at all the whole crowd was chanting, 'We want the mayor, we want the mayor,' which was quite exciting for all those doing the shouting and quite intimidating for everyone else.

In actual fact, none of the children had the faintest idea what the mayor actually looked like. The people peering out of the Town Hall's windows could have sent just about anyone out to try and reason with them and they wouldn't have known the difference. But the large, middle-aged man who eventually stepped out on to the balcony looked exactly how a mayor was meant to look, with a suit, a vague air of self-importance about him and a great chain of office slung around his shoulders, which he'd been wearing for some fancy reception before being so urgently called away.

Most of the chanting stopped, but here and there small pockets of agitation continued. The mayor stared out at the sea of faces and patted the air, to try and quieten things down. He looked utterly stunned. This wasn't what he'd had in mind when he signed up for the job three years earlier. Most of his days were spent attending meetings about the bins or traffic lights, or having his photograph taken for the local newspaper at coffee mornings and sponsored walks.

He kept patting the air until some semblance of order had been established. Then, in a clear, strong voice, so that everyone could hear him, he called out, 'What do you want?'

A skinny boy in a thick pair of glasses shouted, 'Where are the aliens?'

This was quickly followed by other, similar enquiries, such as 'Yeah, where are they?' and 'What've you done with 'em?'

A couple of minutes earlier, when the mayor had been informed that the town's youth were demanding to see him, his first thought was that they must be upset about the quality of their school dinners or the state of their playing fields. But now that he was out on the balcony and had actually heard their concerns he was quite bewildered.

'*What* aliens?' he said at last.

It was just the kind of remark guaranteed to inflame the situation. Most of the crowd immediately started booing. Some children accused the mayor of being a liar, and went on to make some rather personal remarks about how fat and bald he was. And this commotion continued until one voice managed to make itself heard above all the others.

'It's a cover-up!' he cried.

Those few choice words summed up the children's mood quite perfectly: their frustration at the mayor's denial that the aliens even existed, along with their growing suspicion that something deeply sinister was going on behind the scenes. The mayor raised his hands, but it was clear that no amount of patting or shushing was going to bring the crowd to order, so he decided to retreat to the safety of the building and consult some of the many advisers on his staff.

As far as the children were concerned, the facts could not have been plainer: either the aliens had been arrested or the spaceship had taken off again before they'd managed to reach it. Either way, the bigwigs at the Town Hall must have known what had happened and it was, frankly, insulting for them to pretend otherwise. A veil of secrecy had been drawn over the whole alien landing and any communication which had been made with them, but the people at the Town Hall hadn't banked on a spontaneous uprising of the town's younger citizens and their demand to be told the truth.

The mayor's hasty retreat was seen as something of a minor victory and was accompanied by a great deal of cheering and chanting and stamping of feet. Deep in the throng Theodore Gutch was clapping and shouting with the rest of them. Theodore was having the time of his life. He looked around him and thought to himself, 'I *knew* it. I *knew* it was an alien spaceship. We wouldn't all be here if it hadn't been.'

By now, everybody was thoroughly enjoying themselves and a giddy, end-of-term atmosphere had taken hold, when it occurred to Sandra Ward, a girl of eight who played the violin and was already up to Grade Four, that she hadn't seen Miss Bowen, her music teacher, recently. The way in which her thoughts unfolded was probably due in no small part to all the talk of spaceships, along with the fact that Sandra was quite an excitable child. She pictured Miss Bowen walking in the park, and a spaceship hovering high above her. Saw a bright beam of light suddenly pick her out. Miss Bowen shielded her eyes as she looked up. And the next second poor Miss Bowen had been snatched away.

'*Miss Bowen*!' Sandra exclaimed and grabbed the arm of Lucy Gambol, who had a powerful imagination all her own. 'The aliens have abducted *Miss Bowen*!'

It took a little longer for this rumour to circulate than Theodore Gutch's, which wasn't surprising considering the size of the crowd. Miss Bowen was a tall, bespectacled woman in her early forties with an eccentric taste in clothes. She could play the piano, the recorder and just about any other instrument you'd care to put in front of her, including a *crumhorn,* which looked like a walking stick and, when turned upside down and pumped full of air, made a reedy sort of sound which was very popular with the children, as indeed was Miss Bowen herself. In her music lessons they were encouraged to clap and stamp their feet very much like they'd just been clapping and stamping their feet a minute earlier. Her popularity may also have had something to do with the fact that most of her pupils only saw her once a week.

Miss Bowen was something of a free spirit. Rumour had it that she attended belly-dancing lessons and she once

famously burst into tears in front of a class of twenty
whilst playing them a recording of Mendelssohn's Violin
Concerto. So the idea of her being abducted or forced to
do anything against her will greatly upset the children, in a
way that the abduction of, say, Mister Morgan or Bernie
Blakelock, the school janitor, would not have done.

Very soon the chanting had turned into 'Where's Miss
Bowen?' and a few minutes later, once they'd managed to
get the hang of it, 'If there ain't no aliens where is old Miss
Bowen?'

Some of the children were beginning to get quite
emotional. Who knew who might be abducted next? What
Sandra Ward, Lucy Gambol and everyone else had failed
to remember was that Miss Bowen only worked on
Mondays and Fridays, so whilst they were now convinced
she was being held aboard some alien spacecraft she was
actually at home, having a bath and reading a book about
Sri Lanka – a country she hoped to visit the following
year.

Meanwhile, deep in the Town Hall the mayor and his
staff were sitting in emergency session around a vast
mahogany table as Mrs Haworth, the catering lady, went
round with a large pot of strong, sweet tea. One of the
mayor's advisers suggested calling the police, but the
mayor wouldn't have it, knowing that photographs in the
local paper of children being handcuffed and bundled into
police vans would spell an end to his career.

'No,' he said, 'we're going to play it softly-softly. We're going to *negotiate*.' And he appointed his youngest, best-looking assistant to talk to the mob in order to try and establish exactly what their demands were and how far they were prepared to go to ensure that they were met.

Five minutes later, Malcolm Bentley stepped warily out on to the balcony and requested that the crowd nominate three children to meet him on the steps in ten minutes' time.

'We're willing to talk,' he said, and before creeping back to the window, added, 'We've got to find a way through all this,' which was the first positive thing anyone from the Town Hall had said all afternoon and was met with a polite ripple of applause.

Not long after, the locks on the large oak doors at the front of the building could be heard clanking and turning. One of the doors creaked open five or six inches and Malcolm Bentley slipped out, to be met by the three children who had been chosen as representatives – partly due to their skills in diplomacy and partly because they were bigger than everyone else. The man from the Town Hall shook hands with each one of them. Then he produced a notebook from his jacket pocket and pulled the top off a pen between his teeth.

'Now then,' he said, 'what are your demands?'

'The first thing', said Daniel Taylor, 'is *where's the spacecraft?*'

For a moment the young man from the Town Hall

stared, baffled, at Daniel. Then he slowly started scribbling '*Where . . . is . . . spacecraft*' on his pad. He nodded his head as he wrote.

'We're looking into it,' he said.

'Secondly,' said Janet Barber, 'is Miss Bowen safe or has she been experimented on?'

'Miss *Bowen*,' said Malcolm Bentley, writing.

Janet told him how to spell it. 'Our *music* teacher,' she said.

Malcolm continued to write. 'We'll look into that as well,' he said.

When he had finished, Malcolm Bentley waited to see if there were any other demands and the three children briefly wondered if they might add one or two of their own. But they had only been sanctioned to present those already given and didn't want to push their luck, so Daniel Taylor drew the proceedings to a close by saying, 'That's it then,' and nodded his head.

Malcolm Bentley shook hands with all three again, making sure to look each one in the eye, for extra sincerity. 'We're going to need a bit of time,' he said, 'but I'm sure we can work this out.'

Daniel Taylor was not at all impressed with Malcolm Bentley. He thought he was a creepy piece of work. 'Well, put it this way,' said Daniel, 'we're either going to be here or we're going to be at home doing our homework. Where do you think we'd rather be?'

A couple of miles away, in one of the town's grander houses, in one of the better neighbourhoods, the headmistress of the school, Mrs Lambert, was slumped at her kitchen table listening to the radio. She had a mug of tea before her into which she was dunking a succession of ginger biscuits. She had already dunked at least four or five and was telling herself she could dunk just two more and then that would be that or she'd have no room for her baked potato.

She'd once dunked and eaten a whole packet of biscuits in a single sitting – something of which she was neither particularly proud nor especially ashamed. Just as her next biscuit went into her tea the telephone started ringing. She was still busy eating it when she picked up the phone. It was the mayor, who seemed to be doing his best to sound quite calm whilst actually being quite frantic.

He explained how the town square was currently packed with Mrs Lambert's pupils and how they were becoming increasingly restless. Mrs Lambert found this hard to believe. Her pupils could get a little rowdy from time to time but had rarely shown any inclination to actually go on the rampage.

'Are you sure they're *my* lot?' she said, which the mayor didn't find especially helpful.

'We are,' he said. 'They seem to have got it into their heads that an alien spacecraft landed in Lowerfold Park this afternoon and that we're keeping it from them.'

There was a long pause at Mrs Lambert's end of the line.

'That's not true, is it?' she said.

'Of course not,' said the mayor, before pausing himself. 'At least, not that I'm aware of. The thing is, they also seem to think that your music teacher has been abducted.'

The pause at the other end was even longer than the last one.

'Miss *Bowen*?' she said.

The mayor confirmed this.

'Well, why don't you just tell them that they're mistaken?' said Mrs Lambert.

The mayor was beginning to lose his temper. 'I think we've got a bit beyond that,' he said. 'They're all so mad keen on this alien idea that anything we say which they don't like the sound of is seen as part of some great *conspiracy*.'

Eventually Mrs Lambert told the mayor she'd see what she could do and promised to call him back in ten minutes. After she put the phone down she stood in the hall for quite a while, just thinking. She was not a woman who was easily flummoxed. She once had five members of staff all phone in sick on the same Monday morning. She had managed to find a way through that little mess and would find a way through this one. She picked up her address book and flicked through the pages until she came to the letter 'H' for Mrs Holland, another member of her staff and the woman in charge of the arts and crafts cupboard.

'Hello, Barbara?' she said, when the phone was answered. 'It's Molly. Listen, we've got a bit of a situation.' She took a deep breath. 'We're going to need as much tinfoil and papier mâché as you can conjure up.'

Back at the square, the crowd was steadily growing in number as the children on their way home from all the other schools stopped to ask what was going on. They heard about the alien landing, Miss Bowen's disappearance and the whole Town Hall cover-up and all pledged to stand shoulder to shoulder with the demonstrators and demand the release of poor Miss Bowen . . . or the aliens . . . or possibly both.

The children gathered in groups to discuss Important Issues – something they'd never much done in the past. And when their parents finally appeared, wondering where on earth they had got to, and threatened them with dinners gone cold, burnt or fed to the dog, no one moved an inch. Some mothers and fathers tried to drag their child away against their wishes, but the other children linked arms and clung to their trousers and here and there a bit of a scuffle broke out. Tempers frayed, hackles were raised, but in the end the parents relented. To be fair, they didn't have much choice. They were outnumbered, but could see no immediate danger to their children, and if they were completely honest they might have admitted that what bothered them most was the fact that nothing half as exciting had ever happened to them when they were young.

As the evening wore on, flasks of soup and blankets were handed out to the children. If they were going to be staying out all night, their parents reasoned, there was no sense in them getting cold or going hungry. And as darkness fell the children began to congregate around lanterns and candles and their conversations gradually grew more hushed. The stars came out and they lay on their backs, wondering if their music teacher was somewhere up among them and if she was, whether she was enjoying the experience.

The children slipped deeper under their blankets and their eyes grew heavy, until the only thing to be heard were renditions of 'Greensleeves' and 'Cockles and Mussels', sung in honour of their missing teacher, complete with all the harmonies she'd taught them the term before.

The night crept by. The children slept and the earth turned on its axis. Now and then, a child would wake and look around at all its sleeping comrades – would blink, smile, then lie back down again. Until, at last, the sky grew pink and the birds gathered on the Town Hall's window-ledges to warm themselves with the rising sun.

Some of the children were just beginning to stir when the Town Hall door creaked open and Malcolm Bentley slipped out again. He tiptoed over to the sea of bodies, crouched down beside a boy who still wavered somewhere between sleeping and waking and whispered a few words in his ear. Then he moved on, bent down by another child, whispered the same few words, and moved on again, and kept on crouching and whispering before finally creeping back to the Town Hall.

This latest rumour swept slowly through the masses. The children sat up and shook their neighbours. They called out to friends who lay nearby, until one boy got to his feet and made an impassioned announcement.

'The aliens,' he cried. 'They've landed in Lowerfold Park again.'

The children kicked off their blankets and in less than a minute they were on the move again. They all went hammering back up the hill towards the aliens. They raced up Church Street, past the school and through the park gates. They ran beside the bowling green and the tennis courts. Through the gardens and round the duck pond, under the horse chestnuts and out into the playground, where, at long last, they came face to face with the alien spacecraft as it sat on the ground in all its silvery majesty.

The children skidded to a halt. Those at the back pushed forward to try and get a better view. Those at the front resisted – didn't want to get too close.

It wasn't quite as big a spaceship as they'd expected. It was a squat little thing, about ten feet tall with a rounded top. More like a small caravan than a dish or a rocket. And, if truth be told, it was a little lumpy: not half as smooth or sleek as alien spacecraft are meant to be.

But there it sat, as solid and real as the swings and the seesaw, with the sun behind it, which gave it an ominous glow. Nobody said a word. The only sound was the chimes of a church bell, away in the distance.

For quite a while nothing happened. And some of the children began to wonder how long they might have to stand there waiting when, without warning, a hatch in the side of the spacecraft fell open. Not slowly and accompanied by a sinister hissing, like on the telly, but just sort of dropped open and hung there, suspended by what looked like a piece of string.

The children held their breath. Who among them would have the courage to step forward and greet the Martians? Certainly, Daniel Taylor began to wish he'd not been such an eager-beaver the previous day. But as they watched, a foot slowly emerged through the open hatch and stepped on to the tarmac. It wore a silver boot. Then the creature's backside emerged . . . an arm . . . its head. Until the children saw that it was actually Miss Bowen. Miss Bowen setting foot back on Planet Earth.

She may have slipped or simply lost her footing, but to some of the children it seemed as if she'd been rather roughly bundled from the spaceship. An 'Ooh' went up from the crowd of infants. Some assumed she was just a bit dizzy from being whisked up and down the universe. As she regained her balance the hatch was yanked back up behind her. Then, deep within the spacecraft, an engine was started and a plume of exhaust fumes crept out from under it. The children shielded their eyes, expecting some blinding, deafening departure, but instead of lifting off the vehicle revved, clunked into gear then promptly headed off across the playing fields and turned down Danvers Street.

Once the spacecraft was gone the children turned their attention back to their music teacher. She stood completely alone. And, one by one, they began to tiptoe in towards her. The woman looked quite befuddled. Sandra Ward, having been the first to raise the alarm regarding Miss Bowen's abduction, felt quite reasonably that the two of them now had some special kinship and was the first to speak.

'Are you all right, miss?' she said, but before the woman could answer someone else called out, 'Where did they take you?'

Miss Bowen raised a hand to her brow and for a while she just stood there, scanning the horizon.

'She's been brainwashed,' said Theodore Gutch, who considered himself something of an expert on such matters, having read a book on it. 'They've erased her memory.'

And the children feared that their music teacher had been reduced to some sort of zombie – someone who would not be able to tell a crumhorn from a walking stick.

'What's your name, miss?' Daniel Taylor called out softly. 'Do you remember?'

There was a long pause, during which her health and her whole future as a music teacher seemed to hang in the

balance. Then she slowly turned and her eyes finally seemed
to focus.

'Miss *Bowen*,' she said. 'I'm *Miss Bowen*.'

A sigh of relief swept through the crowd. Miss Bowen
was back among them. And the children moved in like a
friendly swarm. They took her hands and looked lovingly
up at her. And very gently, very quietly, they led her back
to the safety of the school.

The girl who collected bones

Everyone likes digging a hole. It's human nature. We like getting our hands dirty. We want to know what's going on down there. Gravediggers, archaeologists and gardeners are all professional hole-diggers, which is why, almost without exception, they are such happy-go-lucky people and always turn up on time for work.

Gwyneth Jenkins liked to dig a hole just as much as the next man. She lived in a cottage on the Gower Peninsula – that bit of land shaped like a piece of jigsaw which hangs off South Wales down into the Bristol Channel. In Gwyneth's opinion, there were plenty of good reasons for living on the Gower, but none better than the fact that you're never far from the sea. Most days of the year she could smell the salt in the air from her doorstep and when she climbed the hill at the bottom of her garden – something she was in the habit of doing two or three times a week – she could see the deep blue bay spread out below her and, when she was right at the top, more water on the other side.

She was sitting on that big, bleak hill one day in early April and thinking about some of the things that had recently been going on in her life. And perhaps it was these thoughts, without her being especially aware of them, that made her dig the heels of her boots into the ground with such grim determination that the grass began to rip and tear away. A patch of dark, damp earth was revealed beneath it. Gwyneth stopped. The soil looked sort of *raw*. And, like any girl with a properly developed sense of curiosity, Gwyneth decided to sit back and carry on digging away at it with the heels of her boots.

Four inches down she turned up a flat, grey stone of quite respectable proportions with a sharp edge along one side. She picked it out and brushed the loose earth off it. Gwyneth thought it was a very handsome stone. She took a firm grip of it between both hands, aimed the sharp edge at the ground and started digging. And within five minutes or so she and that flat stone of hers had dug a fair-sized hole out of the side of the hill.

Gwyneth put her stone to one side and peered down into the dark earth. A lovely loamy smell came up from it. Twists of old root and bits of flint were scattered about the bottom. And various many-legged insects, who were clearly not used to seeing the sunlight, went scurrying about the place. Gwyneth noticed something chalky sticking out from the side of the hole. She got a hold of it and pulled it free. She cleaned it up and examined it more closely. And she found that it was actually a long, thin bone, of about four or five inches – shaped like a shoe-horn or the razor shells that got washed up on the beach below.

It was cold and worn and as dry as a biscuit, and she thought that there was every reason to suppose it might have been lying in the ground for hundreds, if not thousands of years.

'Tired old bone,' she said and sat and looked at it for a couple more minutes. Then she got to her feet, slipped the bone in her jacket pocket and set off down the hill.

When she got back home she dropped the sharp, broad stone she'd used as a home-made shovel into the long grass at the bottom of the garden – the same place she hid any other bits and pieces she picked up on her travels that were either too big or too plain unhygienic to be tolerated inside the house. But she kept the small bone in her jacket pocket and for the rest of the week took it with her wherever she went. When she stood in church and sang, '*Immortal, invisible* . . .' or sat in class and listened to her teacher talking she held it in her hand, deep in her jacket pocket. So whilst she might have *appeared* to be joining in with the hymn-singing or be listening to her teacher, some part of her was always deep in her pocket with that piece of bone keeping warm in the palm of her hand.

It had never been Gwyneth's intention to start a bone collection. She just happened to be up on the hill again the following Sunday and to have her digging stone along with her when she noticed a small boulder which was covered in moss and looked quite interesting. She sized it up and found that by lying on her back and pushing both feet against it she could get it rocking backwards and forwards. And once she'd built up a bit of momentum she managed to roll it right out of the way.

The patch of earth where it had been sitting was brimming with creepy-crawlies. Gwyneth ushered them over to one side and gave the ground a knock with her knuckles. The earth was packed tight – presumably from having such a heavy stone pressing down on it. She sat on the grass, cross-legged, made herself comfortable, took up her digging stone and, like a caveman's daughter, began hacking away at the ground.

It took her a little longer to make any sort of impression than on the previous occasion, but Gwyneth kept steadily at it and after five or ten minutes she'd turned up two smallish bones and a third, curved bone, which looked as if it might once have been part of a larger bone, but was now so old and worn it was impossible to say.

At the end of that second day's dig Gwyneth took her three new bones down to the stream, washed the dirt off them in the ice-cold water and patted them dry in her handkerchief. She had a closer look at them. Then she took out the bone she'd found the previous week, folded her handkerchief around all four bones and carried them home, with them gently rattling against one another, like wooden clothes pegs rattling in a linen bag.

During the week Gwyneth embarked on two more

bone-hunts and quite soon she'd collected so many she
had to carry them around in a metal bucket, which she
kept hidden behind the garden shed. She seemed to have a
bit of a knack for knowing where to find them. Sometimes
she'd simply stop in the middle of nowhere, get out her
digging stone and, in a matter of minutes, unearth another
two or three. Perhaps she just happened to live near a hill
with lots of bones in it. On the other hand, she could
sometimes walk for miles without the least inclination to
stop and have a dig, as if she knew that there was no use
bothering, because there was not the slightest chance of
there being bones down there.

After a couple of weeks, Gwyneth had enough bones to
make herself a simple necklace – a primitive-looking
thing which she created by knotting a piece of string
around a row of some of the smaller bones. She wore it
under her shirt for two days without anyone knowing and
could feel the bones against her skin the whole day long.
The only time it was in danger of being discovered was
when Mrs Madingley called round to see her mother.
Mrs Madingley was a large, rather loud sort of woman
and the moment she spotted Gwyneth she moved in on
her and gave her a powerful hug. Gwyneth could feel all
the air being squashed right out of her and was painfully
aware of the bone necklace getting pressed between the
two of them. When she let her go, Mrs Madingley gave
Gwyneth a little pat on the shoulder, but actually looked

quite worried, as if she was thinking, 'What a bony little girl you are.'

A few weeks later Gwyneth dug up her last bone – a shallow, round thing, like the end of a wooden spoon. Her days of bone digging came to an end just as quickly as they'd started. She had a good bucketful by now, which seemed perfectly adequate. If she needed any more she knew she'd have no trouble finding them. In all her digs, she realized, she'd never given much thought to where the bones actually *came* from. They could have been sheep bones, rabbit bones – even prehistoric bones. But it never seemed particularly important. A bone is a bone, she thought.

Now that she had enough, she got into the habit of carrying her bucket of bones up the hill in the evenings in much the same way that other people take their dog for a walk. One Thursday after school she took her bucket of bones and sat high on the hill looking down over the water. It was still quite warm and, without having made any particular plans to do so, Gwyneth took a handful of bones and began to lay them carefully out on the ground. She put some of the bigger bones at the top and the smaller ones at the bottom. Then she placed some of the straight bones at right angles to each other, with some of the curved bones in between.

The following day she laid them out in a similar fashion, but with the bones lying end to end. The next day she spread them out in an entirely different arrangement.

Each time, when she had finished, she stepped back to see what they looked like. On the Sunday, she laid them out and left a space in the middle. Then she tiptoed in and lay down on the grass among them all.

She lay among the bones with the evening sun warming her face and thought of all the bones in her own body: the bones in her arms, the bones in her rib cage and the small bones in her hands and feet. And she imagined what it must be like to be just bones and to feel the wind and clouds roll endlessly over you. She wondered if that would be a good feeling, or no feeling at all.

Two months earlier, she'd been to visit her grandad. He'd sat in his favourite armchair, but for some reason couldn't seem to make himself comfortable. He kept twisting and turning all the time.

When Gwyneth was small he used to push her in her pram – down to the shops and over to see her auntie. He used to take her swimming in the sea. He was an unusual man, with unusual ideas. But Gwyneth always knew that she could talk to him about absolutely anything and that he would listen and take her seriously.

On that last visit he shuffled and twisted in his armchair as if he was never going to get comfortable ever again. He looked up and shook his head at her.

'My tired old bones,' he said.

Gwyneth's grandad died two days later. Gwyneth never got to see him again. When her mother told her the news Gwyneth burst into tears. She seemed to spend the whole day crying. And whenever she managed to stop herself, the terrible fact that her grandad was gone was always there waiting for her and that would start her crying all over again.

Her mother said that, in time, it might be something she would get used to. But, as Gwyneth told her, it wasn't something she *wanted* to get used to. All she wanted was to have her grandad back.

But now, as Gwyneth lay on the ground among all the bones she'd collected and thought of all the bones in her own arms and ribs and hands and feet, she began to feel quite different from how she'd felt for quite some time.

She felt the evening sun on her face and the breeze sweeping over her. She imagined what she and her bone collection must look like from above. She decided to sit up and, not far away, she saw her grandad. Her old grandad just standing there, looking back at her.

It wasn't a shock or the least bit worrying. It was almost as if she'd expected to find him there. And for a while she just looked at him and thought about him. And eventually she lay back down again.

She lay back among her bones and felt the sun and wind for another few minutes. Then she got to her feet, packed up her bones and went back down the hill. And the following Saturday she took that bucket of bones and buried them in what felt like appropriate places, so that they'd be there, ready and waiting, for anyone else who might be in need of them.

Neither hide nor hair

Finton Carey may have been small, but he was never short of an opinion – a moody, broody sort of boy, who could always be relied upon to say out loud what everyone else was thinking but were wise enough to keep to themselves. When other children saw danger looming and crept around it, young Finn would jump straight in. This earned him a certain respect and caused a great deal of entertainment, but tended to make life more difficult than it might otherwise have been.

Finn's father had left home when he was just a baby. Neither hide nor hair had been seen of the fellow ever since. It didn't bother Finn. Why should he care about a father who clearly didn't care for him? Besides, the house was busy enough with just Finn and his mother – a woman known to have one or two opinions of her own. It had been suggested, more than once, that Finn might have inherited some of his mother's spirit. But Finn was of the firm opinion that being so opinionated was something he'd come up with all by himself.

The two of them argued on a regular basis – often about the most trivial things – but the argument which led to Finn running away came at the end of a long, hard day for the both of them. And with hindsight, it might have been better if two such tired and generally irritable people had been kept well apart.

Finn's mother put his dinner down on the table. Finn surveyed it. A small lump of gristly meat sat hunched and smothered with gravy. A pile of mashed potato towered over it, like Everest. Nearby, a heap of wilted greens relaxed in a pool of its own green juices.

'Eat up,' said Finn's mother. But Finn just kept on looking at his plate.

'I'm not hungry,' he said at last.

His mother looked over at him. Finn could tell that she was already well on her way towards being angry. Someone with less experience might have thought her quite calm, but Finn could see all sorts of tempers and tantrums niggling away at her, just under the skin.

She kept her gaze fixed squarely on him until Finn relented. He sliced off a piece of meat, smeared some mashed potato over it and brought the whole lot up to his mouth. He sat and chewed. He made a big deal of chewing. He chewed as if it might take him the rest of the evening just to get through this one little bit.

'And eat your greens,' said his mother and tapped his plate with her fork.

Finn looked down at the limp green vegetables and felt a couple of choice words take shape in his head. The kind of words which, once said, almost inevitably lead on to other things. He considered trying to keep them where they were, all locked up and unspoken. But some thoughts are like an itch and the only way to scratch them is to let them out.

'Ach, eat the damned things yourself,' he said.

He sat back in his chair and felt a nasty sort of satisfaction flooding through him. He looked over at his mother and waited for her to respond. He didn't have long to wait. All sorts of words came tumbling out of her. Some were unfamiliar. Made-up words, thought Finn, forged in the heat of the moment. Or possibly the kind of words only brought out on special occasions. Either way, Finn knew that he wouldn't be called upon to do any more talking. His mother was doing enough talking for the both of them.

She dragged him upstairs by his ear. It's quite amazing, thought Finn, as he stumbled after her, just how incredibly painful a pinched ear can be. Then he was given a smart little shove so that he went flying into his bedroom, was informed that he was ungrateful, that he had been spoiled rotten and that his mother didn't wish to see anything of him till the following day – which even then might be too soon. Finn's mother was about to shut the door when she hesitated. Finn could tell that she had something on her mind. It was one of those nasty phrases that he was so good at himself. He could see it itching away inside of her. She took a breath, to try and hold it back. Failed.

'It's no wonder your father ran a mile from you,' she said, then slammed the door.

Finn just stood there. At first he felt quite cold. Felt an empty, rushing feeling, as if he was falling from a very great height. But in a couple of seconds he was fairly burning with anger. He could feel its heat roaring in his stomach, as if someone had poured hot coals into him. And as he stood there, quietly raging, he resolved to make his mother pay for those words. He was going to hurt her – hurt her even more than he'd just been hurt himself.

For a while he sat on his bed with his mother's words echoing all around him. Then he stood on a chair and took the suitcase down from the top of the wardrobe – the little case he always packed when he and his mother went away. He opened a drawer and took an armful of socks from it. He didn't know why, but he thought he'd be needing plenty of socks where he was going, along with all sorts of courage and stubbornness. And as he crept about his room, secretly packing, his mother sat down below at the kitchen table with her head in her hands. 'What a horrible thing to say,' she said to herself. 'What a horrible, *horrible* thing to say.'

Finn waited until it was dark then silently opened his bedroom window. He could see the lights of the next village, two or three miles away. He threw his little suitcase so that it landed in the bushes. Then he turned, backed out of the window, hooked a foot around the drainpipe and began to climb down into the dark.

As he walked along the lanes he breathed in the night air and felt how sharp and cold it was inside him. He'd never actually run away from home before, which was quite remarkable considering what a hot-headed boy Finn could be. He'd certainly contemplated running away on any number of occasions. In some ways this just seemed like the perfect opportunity to try it out. One or two aspects of running away made him a little nervous, such as the possibility of being murdered or starving to death. But as he walked along, with his little suitcase full of socks and the moon bright and clear above him, he told himself that any boy who was as stubborn as he was and who was in possession of as many opinions must have a fair chance of making a success of it.

He reached the edge of the woods in less than half an hour. They weren't the sort of woods that children were encouraged to enter, not least because they were so impenetrably deep. Grown men had headed into those woods, loaded up with food and all sorts of maps and compasses and never been seen or heard of again. The only time Finn had ever been in them was with his mother and they had gone no more than fifty or a hundred yards. Certainly, no child had ever been known to go anywhere near them after dark.

It was very strange, but the moment Finn set foot in the woods he felt a powerful change come over him. The smell of the earth and the bark made him feel most welcome. And the sounds were nothing like what he had imagined. The place was alive – ticking and clicking like a vast, natural engine. And as he went deeper into the woods he could feel the trees slowly close behind him, as if they were sealing him in.

He walked for a while – perhaps just twenty minutes – then sat under a huge, tall tree. He opened his little case. In the moonlight he could make out the balls of socks, all huddled together, which for some reason made him feel inconsolably sad. So he closed the lid, placed the case on the ground and carried on walking. And he kept on walking for the rest of the night.

When the sun finally rose the sound of the woods slowly shifted, from the clicking and ticking to a mad sort of chatter, as if half the wood's population was waking whilst the other half was going to bed.

He decided to rest and sat on the ground. The day went by, but went by so slowly. He heard various rustlings and rummagings in the bushes – some close, some quite far away – but apart from a few birds and a great many insects he didn't see anything particularly interesting. The only significant event of that first day came late in the afternoon, when he heard a woman's voice, his mother's voice, calling out his name. He could hear her getting close, then a little closer. Then he heard her slowly fading away.

On the second day he woke up feeling mighty hungry. He'd been crying in the night, he seemed to remember. He knew that it was him who'd been doing the crying, but he'd been half-asleep at the time, so it was almost as if it was someone else and that he was just listening, just as he'd listened to his mother's voice the day before.

He climbed one or two trees and picked some fruit and berries. Those that tasted good he put to one side and finished later. Those that made him sick he made sure not to pick again. And as the days went by he found that he could eat all sorts of things – such as twigs and grass – without them causing him too much trouble. He ate more or less whatever took his fancy and drank the water from the stream.

When the sun went down he wrapped himself in leaves and branches. He would scoop a shallow pit in the ground and pull the twigs and soil right over him. He once tried sleeping up a tree, which was incredibly uncomfortable and he spent the whole night quite convinced that he was going to fall out of it and break his neck.

He got much better at running and climbing and breaking things open. He felt himself slowly change, in all sorts of immeasurable ways. But all the time he kept on moving. Not in any particular direction – just deeper and deeper into the woods.

It may have been a couple of weeks or a couple of months later when he suddenly realized he'd stopped thinking about his mother. He'd just not thought about her in a long, long while. And if his body was changing then so was the way his mind operated. It had been whittled away into something smooth and simple. The only thing that was important was the very next minute. And there was something deeply reassuring in that.

He patched his shoes and clothes with whatever happened to be lying about the place. Folded leaves and bits of bark began to sprout out of him and he began to suspect that if he stood still for long enough the world wouldn't notice and that he would simply disappear. He found a broken branch which, with a little work, looked a bit like the pipes he used to see the old men smoking. And some nights, just before going to bed, he would sit and put his pipe in his mouth, like they used to do. Of course, he had no matches or tobacco. So he just used to chew on it as he looked between the trees which stretched away into the distance, and this seemed to help him relax and prepare for the long, dark night ahead.

He'd been in the woods for quite some time. Perhaps a year or two. His hair was long and tangled and his skin was thick with dirt. He was sitting on a fallen tree, watching the insects crawl across its rotten carcass when he heard a crackle of leaves not far behind him and turned to find a great brown dog, no more than ten feet away. As soon as the dog noticed him it froze. It bared its teeth and started growling. It kept its eyes locked on the boy. But the boy didn't move. He just sat on his old dead tree and watched the dog and started talking. Talked about all sorts of things – most of which made hardly any sense – but in a calm and steady voice. And as he talked the dog slowly stopped its growling, until it finally dropped its head and crept away.

Over the next two or three days he'd occasionally hear the crack of a twig somewhere in the distance or a rustle in the bushes. Then, one night, he scooped himself a bed and pulled some leaves and branches over him and when he woke the following morning he found the dog curled up right next to him. The dog appeared to be fast asleep but the boy felt reasonably sure that it was just pretending. Its eyes were closed but it seemed to be listening to his every move. And from that day forward the dog was a constant companion, with its long brown ears hanging down around its features and its big brown eyes always watching him.

As they tramped through the woods the dog would sometimes go charging off into the bushes, but would always come cantering back within a minute or two. They seemed to get along very well. Two or three times a day they would stop and rest, but on the whole they preferred to keep on moving, even though they had no particular destination in mind.

After a while, the boy found that he and the dog could communicate quite well with one another. In the evenings the boy would get out his home-made pipe and the two of them would sit and talk about whatever came to mind. The dog told the boy how it had been beaten by its owner. Half-way through the story, the dog stopped and stared at the ground and seemed full of shame. He'd been beaten two or three times, the dog said, but the next time it happened he decided he'd had enough so he jumped out of a window and just started walking and ended up in the woods.

The dog asked the boy how he came to be living out in the wild. The boy was surprised to find that he couldn't remember. He remembered having an argument with somebody and, like the dog, making up his mind to run away. But for a boy who had once taken such pride in his opinions he now found that there were great holes in his memory, and what had once seemed so fixed and solid had been all but washed away.

The boy and the dog hardly ever argued. The only thing they disagreed about was what to eat. They never questioned where they were heading or why they were walking. They just kept putting one foot in front of the other until the sun started to slip from the tops of the trees, at which point they would stop and try to find somewhere dry to spend the night.

One evening they were sitting and talking when the boy asked if the dog had ever had a name. The dog sat and thought for a moment. He said he felt sure he used to have one but couldn't recall it. Anyway, he said, it was a name given him by his cruel owner, so he had no wish to be called by it.

'What about you?' said the dog. 'You must have had a name.'

The boy looked suddenly troubled.

'I did,' he said, 'but I've forgotten it.'

The fact that he'd forgotten his name bothered the boy a great deal more than it bothered the dog. The boy sat and chewed it over, until the dog told him not to worry about it. Then they lay down, pulled the leaves around them and tried to get some sleep.

A couple of months later, they were walking along when the boy was suddenly swamped by a peculiar feeling. He stopped and looked all around him. The dog asked what was the matter, but the boy wasn't sure. The trees in that particular part of the wood seemed oddly familiar. As if he had visited them in a dream. They walked on for a little while longer, then the boy suddenly stopped again. He turned and pointed to a huge tree in the distance.

'I know that tree,' he said.

The boy and the dog went over to it. When they got there the boy started rooting around in the bushes beneath it.

The dog asked him what he was looking for.

'I don't know,' said the boy.

He picked up a stick and began to hack away at the bracken and finally found a small suitcase tucked away in a clutch of ferns. The sides of the case were all stained and sodden. Its lid was covered with a thick green coat of moss. He crouched down, pushed back the latches and the locks sprang open. He lifted the lid and found the balls of socks inside.

The dog stuck his nose in the case and had a sniff around.

'Are they yours?' said the dog.

The boy looked quite baffled. 'I think they must be,' he said.

They sat by the tree for a while. The boy felt as if he had too many thoughts for his head to handle. He felt as if all the trees which had been keeping him secret were slowly being stripped away. He looked up and nodded into the distance.

'That's where I come from,' he said.

The dog looked in the same direction. 'Are you going back there?' he said.

The boy kept staring into the distance.

'I haven't decided,' he said at last.

They crept up to the edge of the trees, waited until it was dark, then waited a little while longer. Then they got to their feet and said their goodbyes. The boy knew what the dog wanted to know, without it even asking.

'When you're tired of waiting, go,' he said.

The boy set off down the lane. With every step another memory seemed to come to meet him and another part of his past fell into place. For the first time in years he knew where he was going. He wasn't sure that he liked it. His feet seemed to be slowly leading him back home. And within half an hour he was standing in the dark, looking up at the cottage where he'd spent so much of his young life.

He opened the gate, slipped into the garden and tiptoed over to a window where a light was shining. And there, sitting in her old armchair, was the boy's mother. She was sleeping and looked much older than the boy remembered, but she was his mother just the same.

He wanted to rush in and throw his arms around her. Wanted to tap at the window and wake her from her dreams. But he found that he couldn't. He couldn't tear himself away from the life he'd made for himself in the woods and go back to his old life. So he just stood there, like a ghost at the window, watching his mother silently sleep.

He ran back down the lanes with all the memories rushing around him. The night seemed a great deal wilder and more frightening than any he'd spent among the trees. When he reached the edge of the wood the dog crept out to meet him. He studied the boy, to try and work out what was going on inside of him.

'Are you all right?' said the dog eventually.

The boy nodded. And without another word, they turned and disappeared back into the trees.

Crossing the river

A 'hearse' is basically a large black car for ferrying dead people from one place to another, with big windows down both sides so that you can see the coffin, and a handful of men in black suits, sitting bolt upright, to keep it company.

Hearses tend to go very slowly. Hearses just sort of glide along. And as they make their way down the streets they bring a melancholy air along with them, like a big, black cloud blocking out the sun.

It is considered bad manners for other cars to honk their horns or flash their lights at hearses to tell them to get a move-on, just as it is considered bad manners to knock over old ladies or laugh out loud in libraries. When you see a hearse with a coffin on board it is customary to remove your hat and stand to attention while it passes. If you're not wearing a hat then you should bow your head. This is called 'showing respect for the dead', but, in truth, what you're really showing respect for is Death itself.

The Woodruffs were perfectly suited to undertaking. Old Man Woodruff had a face like a bloodhound and his three sons – Vernon, Earl and Leonard – were about as miserable a bunch of men as you could hope to meet. The

Woodruffs hadn't been the happiest family to begin with.
Then Lillian Woodruff, wife and mother, died before her
sons had finished growing up, which made a hard life even
harder and left a stain of sadness on all four of them.

Old Man Woodruff liked to sit in the passenger seat. He
considered it his right as the family elder and reckoned his
dour demeanour helped set the right tone. His sons
weren't particularly bothered where they sat, although
Vernon did most of the driving, which meant that Earl and
Leonard usually ended up in the back.

When they were out in the car it was generally felt that
they should look straight ahead and be as impassive as
possible. Nose-picking, smiling, yawning and face-pulling
were all considered inappropriate. If they passed an old
friend in the street, they confined themselves to a curt nod
of the head or discreet little wink and any conversation in the
hearse itself was conducted out of the corner of the
mouth, with a minimum of expression.

But the Woodruffs certainly knew what they were doing.
Over the years they must have delivered several hundred,
if not thousands, of corpses to their final resting place.
When people suddenly found themselves in possession of
a dead body their first call was often to the Woodruffs. In
certain circumstances a bit of glumness is just the job. But
such a reputation was no comfort to Old Man Woodruff
on that fateful Friday, when they were out in the country
carrying some old-timer to his funeral and Vernon checked

his rear-view mirror and found that the car with the old-timer's family in it, which was meant to be following, was nowhere to be seen.

'Hmm,' said Vernon.

'What do you mean – *hmm*?' said his old dad.

'The *mourners*,' said Vernon. 'They ain't there.'

If they hadn't had so many years' experience behind them Earl and Leonard might have been sorely tempted to look over their shoulder, but all four Woodruffs kept looking straight ahead, despite the fact that there was no one watching them. Vernon gently brought the hearse to a halt and looked hopefully into his mirror, but the car containing the dead man's family failed to materialize.

'You great nelly,' said Leonard from the back seat. 'How could you lose 'em?'

Vernon hadn't the foggiest idea.

'They must've taken a wrong turn,' he said.

Their father was shaking his head most gravely.

'This is a bad day,' he said. 'Very bad. I knew it the minute I stepped out of bed.'

The Woodruffs sat and waited in that country lane for a good five minutes, without a single other vehicle rolling into view. Their only company was a couple of cows who slowly ambled over and poked their heads through the hedgerow to see what was going on.

Eventually, Old Man Woodruff exploded.

'This is *ridiculous*,' he said, and instructed Vernon to

drive on. 'We'll just have to catch up with them at the church.'

And so they pressed on, down narrow roads which grew steadily narrower, on to lanes which were so rough and bumpy they were barely worth the name. Half-way down a steep hill one of the hearse's wheels bounced in and out of a pot-hole with such a thump that the coffin leapt up, as if the dead man inside was having seconds thoughts about being buried and had decided to call the whole thing off. Earl and Leonard weren't remotely troubled by it. They'd been over bigger bumps in the past and, without uttering a word, they both raised a calming hand over their shoulder to stop the coffin hitting them in the back of the head.

Thick brambles began to scratch and screech down the sides of the hearse. Old Man Woodruff was shaking his head again.

'We should've checked the *route*,' he said, with great feeling. 'We should've stuck to churches that we actually *know*.'

Vernon's confidence, regarding where they were and where they were going, rose and fell just like the lanes along which they travelled. There were also odd moments in which he admitted (if only to himself) that he had no idea where on earth they were. He would have had more hope of finding his way back on to a road he actually *recognized* if he'd been at the wheel of a car which could have been more easily turned around. The fact that the hedgerows were ten feet tall and prevented him from getting his bearings did nothing but make matters worse.

After wandering round that maze of lanes for a further twenty minutes they finally came out into a clearing on a hillside. Vernon stopped the car. Down to their right they could see the great, wide river. On the far side they could see the roofs of a village and, in their midst, a church steeple pointing towards the heavens.

'There it is,' said Vernon. 'That's the church we're after.'

The hearse slowly filled up with an ominous silence.

'Where's the bridge?' said Len.

Vernon jabbed a thumb over his left shoulder. 'About ten miles thataway,' he said.

Old Man Woodruff, having only just managed to pull himself together, promptly fell apart again. He dropped his head into his hands and began muttering darkly. Earl was getting royally sick of his dad's incessant carping and moaning and was about to tell him to get a grip when Leonard spotted a cottage right down by the river.

'Right,' he said. 'Everyone out.'

Harold Digby had just finished a plateful of ham and eggs and three slices of bread and butter and was sitting in his favourite chair with a mug of tea in his hand. He was looking forward to a little nap once the tea was inside him. He liked a little snooze after a bit of food. He once closed his eyes about half-past twelve and didn't come round until getting on for three o'clock and he was wondering what the chances were of him pulling off a record-breaking snooze this afternoon when someone suddenly started banging on his front door.

'Isn't that just ruddy typical?' Harold said to himself.

He put down his mug of tea and got to his feet. He straightened his hair, in case it was anyone important, and opened the door to find four sinister-looking fellows all dressed up in black suits, with a coffin resting on their shoulders.

'Are you the ferrymaster?' the old one asked him.

Poor Harold felt quite faint. He somehow got it into his head that Death had come a-calling. That it planned to toss him in its coffin and take him away.

He swallowed hard. There seemed to be no point in lying. 'I am,' he said.

'Good,' said the old fellow. 'We've got some ferrying for you to do.'

Harold was greatly relieved that his days on earth were not yet over and that he had any number of years still left to set things straight. All the same, he let it be known that he was far from happy taking a dead body in his boat, even if it was a dead body wrapped up in a wooden box.

'Four's usually the limit,' he said, as he led the Woodruffs and their coffin down the rickety old pier to where his boat was tethered.

'Think of him as luggage,' said Earl, which seemed to shut him up for a while.

Getting the coffin on to the boat wasn't a problem. The problem was finding a place for everyone to sit. The coffin fitted quite snugly across the two crosspieces but the boat wasn't particularly wide, so the only way to get everyone on board was for them to squeeze in around it and hang over the sides.

Old Man Woodruff insisted he sit up front, just like in the car. The others tried several different ways of distributing themselves about the boat, without success. And all the time, their dad kept saying how they were late and that people would be waiting, until finally Harold Digby took charge of the situation and announced that as he'd have to sit astride the coffin to do the rowing, the only sensible thing was for the others to do the same.

Which is how they came to set sail with all five of them straddling the coffin, like some gruesome fairground ride. The moment they left the quay everybody fell silent. The Woodruffs were concentrating with all their might. The whole arrangement was a bit top-heavy, but Mister Digby assured everyone that as long as they sat quite still he'd have them over the other side in no time at all.

They were doing very well until they got about half-way over, with Mister Digby rowing and facing back towards his cottage and the Woodruffs facing the other way. They were travelling about as smoothly and quietly as they did in their hearse when Leonard started shifting and squirming.

'What's going on back there?' said Old Man Woodruff.

'It's my underpants,' said Leonard. 'They're riding right up.'

Everyone told him to sit tight until they'd got where they were going. But Leonard couldn't think of anything else. He lifted his backside until it was clear of the coffin, hooked a thumb under the offending piece of underpant and yanked it clear. But when he sat back down he misjudged his landing and slipped – quite violently – to the right. The others leant to the left, to try and compensate, but overdid it. The boat tilted one way, then the other, and with each swing it gained momentum, until it finally went right over and deposited the Woodruffs, Harold Digby and the coffin into the river.

A terrible splashing and thrashing ensued, as each man fought to keep his head above the water. But as any lifeguard worth his salt will tell you, it is one thing to swim in nothing but a pair of trunks and quite another to do so fully clothed. Leonard, Earl and Vernon weren't particularly good swimmers. Even Mister Digby was not as good as one might expect. But Old Man Woodruff had never learnt a stroke and all he could think to do was kick his feet and claw at the water.

'Doggy-paddle . . . doggy-paddle,' he said out loud, to try and give himself some encouragement.

The boat was upside-down and already twenty yards

from them. The only thing left floating that they could get
a hold of was the coffin and once they got a hold of it they
weren't about to let it go.

The coffin rocked and bobbed as each man got an arm
around it, but it never threatened to let them down. When
all five of them were attached they took a minute to clear
their lungs and catch their breath.

'Are you all right, dad?' said Leonard.

He said he was, but that the sooner they were out of
the water the better. And without anyone in particular
suggesting it one or two of them started flapping their feet,
and soon all five of them were slowly propelling the coffin
the rest of the way.

'Kick,' said Old Man Woodruff, who was suddenly an
expert swimmer. 'Kick out with your feet.'

When they got to the other bank they stood around for a
while, cursing and dripping. And when the Woodruffs had
finally agreed some sort of compensation with Mister
Digby and done their best to smarten themselves up a bit,
they lifted the coffin back on to their shoulders and headed
up the hill.

There was a fair-sized crowd waiting for them. As they
approached the church an old lady, who looked most upset
and was therefore most likely to be the dead fellow's
widow, headed over towards them. They came to a halt at
the church gates and the old woman looked them up and
down. Their suits were sopping wet and their hair was

plastered to their heads. As they stood there, small pools of water gathered around their feet.

'Where on earth have you been?' she asked Old Man Woodruff.

He cleared his throat and mustered as much authority as he could in the circumstances.

'We checked the records, ma'am,' he said, 'and found no sign of a christening. We thought it best to baptize him – just to be sure.'

The button thief

Thelma Newton wasn't much more than a toddler. The very top of her was only a couple of feet higher than the very bottom. She hoped to do some growing up later on in life, but in the meantime she had a habit of wearing at least two or three jumpers, which made her look quite chunky, and when she wore her favourite coat on top of them she was almost as wide as she was tall.

Her Auntie Blanche bought her that coat. In the winter Thelma wore it fully-buttoned, with the hood up. In the summer she wore it open, to let a little air circulate. She was uncommonly fond of it and on a couple of occasions had even worn it in bed, until her parents happened to notice and insisted she put on her pyjamas, like any normal girl.

One Sunday Thelma was out walking with her father, with her hood pulled up to keep her ears warm and a pair of clumpy boots to stop her sinking in the mud. They walked over the tops to have a look at the reservoir and on their way home passed a field with an old horse standing in the middle, idly chewing at the grass. Thelma had once seen a film about a girl who owned a horse. The two of them were forever galloping off into all sorts of adventures and, for a while, Thelma had dreamed of owning a horse herself.

Thelma's father, thinking that his daughter still had a bit of a soft spot for horses, tried to call the old nag over, which he did by hanging over the fence, rubbing his fingers together and making a sort of clacking noise out of the corner of his mouth. It took a while, but the old horse finally decided to amble over. Thelma's father looked so pleased with himself at having got it moving that Thelma felt rather obliged to pretend to be pleased herself, even though she'd given up on the whole idea of owning a horse and having horsey adventures several months before.

The old horse certainly wasn't in any sort of hurry. It just kept ambling along in their general direction, at its own leisurely pace and all the clacking and rubbing-together of fingers from Thelma's dad didn't seem to make much difference at all. When it finally arrived Thelma saw what a truly mangy old beast they were dealing with. It looked about a hundred and fifty years old. A stump of bristly hair stuck up between its ears, like a toilet brush, and various other whiskers hung out of its ears and nose and chin. It tupped Thelma's dad out of the way with its big old head, then leant over the fence, right down to where little Thelma was standing, to see what was going on down there.

'Don't worry, Thelma,' her father told her, as if he knew the first thing about horses. 'It just wants to have a sniff at you.'

Thelma's father could have claimed to have been at least half-right, because once the horse's head was down at

Thelma's level it started snuffling and snorting with its big old nostrils and gave Thelma's head and shoulders such a thorough going-over she could feel the heat of its horse-breath blasting all about her and its whiskers as they dragged across her face.

Thelma wasn't particularly enjoying having the horse's head so close to her. For a start, it was about ten times bigger than her own head. It also had the most disgusting-smelling breath. It smelt as if it had spent the morning smoking a pipe or working its way through a sack of old onions. But Thelma gritted her teeth and let the nag continue to sniff her. Another few seconds and it'll all be over, she told herself.

The horse dropped its head another six or eight inches so that it was right down in front of Thelma's and its mad old eyes stared deep into hers. It peeled its lips right back and showed Thelma the many yellow teeth which were mouldering away in there. Then it made a sudden lunge for the top button on Thelma's coat, latched its teeth around it and yanked its big old head right up into the air.

Thelma's coat left the ground with Thelma still in it. Her dad did what most dads would do in the circumstances and started shouting and waving his arms about. Thelma watched him getting smaller and smaller as she went higher and higher. The horse jiggled her up and down and swung her from side to side just like a rag doll and Thelma was quite convinced that at any moment the horse was going to take a big bite out of her, like a muffin or a piece of pie.

She hung in the air for quite a while and might have hung there a good while longer if the threads which held her button to her coat hadn't finally broken. She fell to the ground – a distance of some four or five feet, which might not sound very far to taller people but to a girl of Thelma's modest proportions felt like a mighty long way.

When all the falling was finally over she landed flat on her back, which knocked the wind right out of her. Then the horse went galloping off across the field, kicking its back legs in the air in celebration and making an awful high-pitched whinny, which sounded suspiciously like horse-laughter of the cruellest kind. Thelma lay in the mud until her father put her back on her feet and checked no bones were broken. To her credit, she didn't cry or make a fuss. She was too bewildered. But when she looked down at her coat all she saw were a couple of threads sticking out where her top button should be.

'He's eaten my button,' she said. Then promptly burst into tears.

Back home, Thelma's parents did their best to console her. They gave her a bath, put her to bed and generally showered her with sympathy. As she slept, her mother cleaned the mud off her coat, and over breakfast the next morning Thelma was assured that they would find a replacement for the button which the horse had so ruthlessly snatched away. But none of the shops they

visited seemed to stock anything like it. All the buttons
they were offered were the wrong size or the wrong sort of
colour. And, besides, Thelma knew very well where the
missing button had got to and felt that a bit more effort
should be put into trying to get that one back.

Thelma's parents explained how the button would have
to '*work its way right through the horse's body*' and that the
only way of finding it would be to go round the field and
check all the horse's '*business*'. The two of them pulled
such faces simply describing the process it was fairly evident
that, no matter how much Thelma begged them, they were
not about to take her back up to that horse's paddock to
spend the afternoon poking about in its dung.

So on the Tuesday young Thelma took matters into her
own hands. She rummaged around in the garage and
found her dad's old motorcycle gloves which came right
up to her armpits. Then, at the next available opportunity,
she put on her coat, with the threads still poking out where
the button had been wrenched from it, and headed off
towards the field.

Nobody seemed particularly bothered by the sight of
such a small girl marching up the road without an adult.
Perhaps the big gloves gave her some sort of authority. She
certainly strode along with plenty of purpose. And within
twenty minutes Thelma was back at the field with the old
horse in it.

It was standing some distance away and appeared to be

looking in a different direction, but Thelma had the feeling
that it knew very well that she was there. She clambered
up on to the fence and looked around the field for horse
dung. She could see at least twenty piles of the stuff, but
decided that the most sensible idea would be to start with
the wettest, freshest specimens, as they'd be the most
recent and most likely to have her precious button hidden
in them somewhere.

As she prepared to climb into the field with that mad
old horse she did her best to convince herself that by
remaining alert at all times she could avoid being picked
up, jiggled about and dropped in the mud again. She
would keep an eye on it at all times, she told herself, and
if it made the slightest move in her direction she'd run
like the clappers. She wasn't particularly tall but she was
a good little runner and if that horse decided to come
anywhere near her she'd be out of that field in a flash.

She'd got one leg through the fence and was easing the
rest of herself after it when someone suddenly started
screaming. Thelma turned to find an old lady running
towards her. One hand was waving a rolled-up brolly. The
other clutched a small dog to her chest.

'No you don't, young lady,' the old woman called out, as
she hurtled towards her. 'No sir. No siree.'

By the time Thelma managed to extract herself from
the fence the old lady was standing right over her. Her eyes
were wild and she was shaking her head as if something

unpleasant was rattling around inside it.

'No sir, little missy,' she said. 'You climb in there and that . . .' She paused to find the right word. '. . . that *monster* will bounce you from one end of the field to the other. Just for *sport*.'

Of course, Thelma had her own, first-hand experience of the vicious animal and would have been only too happy to share it, but the old woman was too busy talking to listen to anyone else. She had a long list of complaints regarding that horse and was determined to work right through it. As she ranted and raved Thelma noticed how the horse slowly made its way over and came to a halt less than ten yards away. It stood and listened most intently – seemed to be quite enjoying the show.

The month before, the old lady was saying, that blasted horse had very nearly done for her darling Pickles. The dog had wandered into the field, the horse had got a hold of it by its collar and proceeded to swing it round and round above its head. As she described the scene the old lady bared her teeth and rolled her head round and round on her shoulders. The dog, which was still clutched to her bosom, seemed thoroughly sickened at being reminded of the incident. The horse, on the other hand, threw its head back and snorted with derision and seemed quite delighted to hear the story again.

'She'll hardly walk at all these days,' the old lady confided. 'At least, not near here she won't. I have to pick her up.'

The old lady looked down at her dog and tickled it under its chin to try and cheer it up, but the dog was completely lost in its own little world of worry. Thelma took advantage of the break in the old woman's monologue to recount her own tale of horse argy-bargy.

'He ate my button,' she said and showed the old lady where it used to be.

The old lady studied the remaining threads and shook her head. Then she turned, looked over at the horse and gave it a scowl of the greatest severity. Thelma scowled at the horse herself. But the dog, being of a more nervous disposition, couldn't bring itself to actually look at the animal and kept its eyes averted.

When they'd finished scowling, the old lady asked Thelma if she'd reported the incident. Thelma had to admit that she had not. She hadn't realized there was a place where one reported such incidents.

'Well, you must report it to its *owner*,' the old lady told her. 'Old Mister Edwards.'

In truth, it hadn't occurred to Thelma that the horse might actually have an owner. It seemed so arrogant and so thoroughly unregulated that she couldn't imagine it answering to anyone other than itself. So it came as no real surprise to hear the horse's owner described in the most pathetic and weak-spirited terms. All the same, the old lady insisted that lodging a complaint with him was the very least one should do in the circumstances and offered

to accompany Thelma to the Edwards farmhouse straightaway. So they set off down the lane and after a while the
old lady put her dog down and it did a bit of walking, but
all the time it kept glancing over its shoulder, as if a horse
might suddenly grab it by its collar and start tossing it
about the place again.

At the gate to the farm the old lady said goodbye and she
and her dog carried on their way, with the old lady using her
rolled-up brolly as a walking stick and her dog looking as if
it wouldn't be happy until it was back home in front of the
fire. Thelma approached the farmhouse and it quickly
became apparent that the whole place was teetering on the
verge of rack and ruin. The roof of the barn was all sunk in
the middle and two or three of the cottage's windows were
broken and had been boarded up with bits of wood. A few
scrawny-looking hens picked over the ground and Thelma
carefully made her way between them. When she reached
the safety of the doorstep she knocked on the door and after
a while it was opened by an old man who was wearing a pair
of worn-out overalls. What was left of his hair clung to his
head in a sort of froth. Long grey socks hung off his feet in
great flaps and folds. He was, thought Thelma, rumpled at
both ends.

Mister Edwards wasn't used to having people of Thelma's
size knocking on his front door. In fact, he wasn't used to
having callers of any sort.

'Can I help you?' he said, looking down at her.

Thelma could see no point in beating about the bush. She turned and pointed back up the lane.

'That horse of yours . . .' she said. 'He ate my button.'

To support her claim she pointed to her coat, where the button had once resided.

'He nearly broke my blummin' neck,' she said.

The farmer winced, as if he'd stubbed his toe or slammed a door on his finger. Then he shook his head in a sorry sort of way.

'He's a ruddy *menace*, that horse,' he said. 'If you let him anywhere near you he'll 'ave you.' The shaking of the head turned effortlessly into nodding. 'And, oh yes – he'll 'ave your buttons. Every one.'

These words of warning came a bit too late for little Thelma. The memory of the attack came flooding back to her and she felt her eyes filling up with tears. The farmer could see the little girl was upset but wasn't sure what he was meant to do about it, so he just continued to run his old horse down.

'He's got a ugly nature,' he said. 'Very ugly. And got more buttons in him than an 'aberdasherers.'

Apparently, it wasn't just buttons that took the horse's fancy. Anything not properly attached to a person seemed to be in danger of disappearing. The horse had snatched and swallowed several earrings, an old man's spectacles and, on at least one occasion, a dummy right out of a baby's mouth.

'He has a special compartment, you see,' the farmer told Thelma and patted his own stomach, round to the right. 'That's where he keeps his booty. And when he pleases, he can cough himself up any old badge or button. To show it off to the world.'

The theft of the dummy, the farmer reckoned, had taken place six or seven years earlier and the boy was now quite grown up, but whenever he happened to pass by, the horse would still bring the dummy back up and proudly display it between its yellow teeth.

'You know,' the farmer said, '. . . in order to *taunt* the boy.'

Thelma was amazed that an animal would go out of its way to be so callous. She was also amazed that such behaviour could go unpunished.

'You should put a sign up,' she said. 'To warn people.'

'You're right,' the farmer conceded. 'I keep meaning to. But I never seem to find the time.'

For a while Mister Edwards just stood on his doorstep, as if he had run out of things to say on the subject. Thelma could see that he was genuinely sorry and she appreciated, perhaps better than anyone, what sort of miserable, bad-tempered horse he had on his hands. But she could also see that, at this rate, the farmer would do precisely nothing to help her, so she told him, in no uncertain terms, that she thought the least he could do was offer to try and get her button back.

167

'You're right. Yes, I should,' he said, still quite hopeless. 'He's never returned anything up to now. But, yes. Let's go up and I'll have a word.'

So, once he'd found his jacket and managed to tuck all his loose socks into a pair of wellingtons, Mister Edwards led the way through the chickens and back up the lane. As they walked along Thelma asked what the horse was *called*, thinking that knowing its name might make it a little less intimidating, but the farmer started shaking his head again.

'I've tried,' he said, rather wearily. 'Tried all sorts of names on him. But he wouldn't wear 'em. No, not a one.'

After this exchange Mister Edwards sank into such sombre contemplation Thelma felt that it would be rude to interrupt, so the rest of the journey passed in total silence, except for Mister Edwards's occasional grunt or groan.

As soon as they reached the gate the old horse began to make its way over. It spotted Thelma and fixed its mean old eyes on her. To be more precise, it fixed its eyes on her five remaining buttons. The farmer could see what the horse was after and shielded Thelma from it and made sure she stood a few yards back. He took a moment to prepare himself and when he finally spoke he did so directly to the animal, as if talking to an aged relative who'd been caught shoplifting and brought home by the police.

'This little girl tells me you've ate her button,' he said.

The horse said nothing.

'Is that true?' the farmer said. 'Have you stole a button off her?'

Again, the horse declined to comment and went so far as to turn away. It held its head up in the air in a lofty fashion, as if any accusations or criticism would simply bounce right off it. It was clear to Thelma that the horse wasn't about to own up to anything, but the farmer persisted and slowly worked himself up into quite a state.

'You mean old nag,' he said. 'You've stole this little girl's button. I *know* it. Now you just cough it right back up.'

The horse turned right around, so that its back was towards the farmer and gazed off towards the horizon, as if considering going there on holiday. Thelma had never seen such wilful ignorance. But Mister Edwards persevered and was about to launch into another tirade when the horse lifted its tail and let loose a blast of wind which was so strong and suffocating it nearly knocked the farmer off his feet.

Thelma was standing some distance away but still caught the edge of it. The merest whiff was enough to make her head spin and bring tears to her eyes. Poor Mister Edwards, however, had taken the full force and staggered about, as if he had just been punched in the stomach. He put his head between his knees to try and stop himself falling over and for a minute Thelma thought he was actually going to be sick. When he finally stood up straight – or as straight as any old farmer is likely to manage – his face was riddled not just with pain but humiliation.

'You horrible, *horrible* animal,' whispered Mister Edwards, and without another word, either to the horse or Thelma, he stumbled off down the lane.

The horse turned and watched him disappear. It seemed almost disappointed. But as soon as its owner was out of sight it looked back over at young Thelma and flashed its evil eyes at her. She was obviously the horse's last hope of a little entertainment, but Thelma shook her head at the horse and set off home herself.

As she walked along, the horse walked beside her with the fence between them. It kept glancing over towards her and Thelma wondered if she couldn't perhaps detect in the horse's attitude the merest trace of regret. But right at the point where Thelma's path veered away from the field, the horse cantered ahead, stopped, turned to face her and proceeded to pull the most extraordinary face. It stuck its tongue out, its eyes rolled back in their sockets and for a moment Thelma thought that perhaps it was building up to some almighty sneeze. Then it coughed – a single, bone-jangling clearing of the throat which started out deep down inside it and slowly developed into a rattling wheeze. The horse stretched its neck out towards the ground and jiggled its head up and down for several seconds. Then, after it had regained a little composure, it took a step in

Thelma's direction. It seemed to wink before peeling its lips back. And there, clamped between its yellow teeth, was Thelma's button.

Thelma instinctively reached out towards it, but the horse pulled its head away. And once it was sure that Thelma had actually seen the button, it flicked its head back and gulped the button back down again.

The horse laughed out loud but Thelma was absolutely livid. 'You *bully*,' she said, 'You big fat ugly *bully*,' and shook her little fist at it.

The horse laughed long and hard – laughed for what felt like several minutes. Its wickedness knew no bounds. And whenever it paused to catch its breath and saw the look of indignation on Thelma's face it started laughing even harder, until it fell into a paroxysm of wheezing and whinnying and generally succumbed to horse-hysteria.

Thelma was ready to leave the horse to its self-indulgence when its celebrations suddenly ceased. The horse stood stock-still with a puzzled look on its face, closely followed by a look of profound alarm. Its mouth fell open and its eyes grew wide. Something seemed to have got lodged deep in its breathing apparatus and in a matter of seconds the animal was coughing and frantically fighting for its breath.

Its whole body clenched and rocked backwards and forwards, as it tried desperately to clear its gullet. It started retching and choking and writhing-about. And this continued until, with one great lunge of its head, a huge torrent of buttons came gushing out over the fence in a button rainbow which forced Thelma to skip to one side to get out of the way.

A single, powerful snort fired one last button out of a nostril. Then the horse hung its head over the fence and stared wretchedly down at what it had just brought up. Thelma bent over the pile of buttons which nestled in the grass, covered in a thick gloop of horse-spittle. There must have been well over a hundred buttons there – all different sizes and colours. Among them Thelma spotted a pair of old-fashioned spectacles, a couple of earrings and a baby's dummy.

She pulled her dad's motorcycle gloves right up to her armpits and began to carefully pick through the button mountain, with the horse still watching. And there, deep in the pile, she found her own precious button. She picked it out, wiped it on her trousers and lifted it up between her finger and thumb.

She turned and showed it to the horse.

'Hah!' she said.

Once Thelma got the button back home and it had been thoroughly washed in hot soapy water, her mother sewed it back where it belonged. Then Thelma put her coat back on, buttoned it up to her throat and proudly marched around the garden, as if she'd just had a medal pinned to her chest.

The following Sunday, at Thelma's request, she and her parents spent the morning making their own home-made signposts. In the afternoon they took them up to the field and erected them at regular intervals – close enough to the fence so that it was clear to whom they were referring but not so close that the horse could get its teeth into them.

The horse watched Thelma hammer them home and looked thoroughly sickened.

There was no mistaking the information the signs imparted.

BEWARE.
BUTTON THIEF.

they said.